W9-BEK-283

THE

PERIPATETIC

COFFIN

AND OTHER STORIES

ecco

An Imprint of HarperCollins *Publishers*

THE
PERIPATETIC
COFFIN

and Other Stories

Ethan Rutherford

Grateful acknowledgment is made to the following publications in which these stories first appeared, in slightly different form: "The Peripatetic Coffin" in *American Short Fiction;* "Summer Boys" in *One Story;* "John, for Christmas" in *Ploughshares;* "Camp Winnesaka" in *Faultline;* "The *Saint Anna*" in *New York Tyrant;* "The Broken Group" in *Fiction on a Stick;* "Dirwhals!" on FiveChapters.com.

This book is a work of fiction. The characters, incidents, and dialogue are drawn from the author's imagination and are not to be construed as real. Any resemblance to actual events or persons, living or dead, is entirely coincidental.

THE PERIPATETIC COFFIN AND OTHER STORIES. Copyright © 2013 by Ethan Rutherford. All rights reserved. Printed in the United States of America. No part of this book may be used or reproduced in any manner whatsoever without written permission except in the case of brief quotations embodied in critical articles and reviews. For information address HarperCollins Publishers, 10 East 53rd Street, New York, NY 10022.

HarperCollins books may be purchased for educational, business, or sales promotional use. For information please write: Special Markets Department, HarperCollins Publishers, 10 East 53rd Street, New York, NY 10022.

FIRST EDITION

Designed by Suet Yee Chong

Library of Congress Cataloging-in-Publication Data has been applied for.

ISBN 978-0-06-220383-0

13 14 15 16 17   OV/RRD   10 9 8 7 6 5 4 3 2 1

For MH & LL

"Good morning," said Emily politely.

"Smells like an earthquake," said Margaret, and dressed.

—Richard Hughes, *A High Wind in Jamaica*

"And the flowers are *still* standing!"

—Dr. Peter Venkman

contents

the peripatetic coffin

1

summer boys

27

john, for christmas

49

camp winnesaka

87

the *saint anna*

107

the broken group

137

a mugging

165

dirwhals!

185

THE

PERIPATETIC
COFFIN

AND OTHER STORIES

the
peripatetic coffin

The sound of iron walls adjusting to the underwater pressure around you was like the sound of improbability announcing itself: a broad, deep, awake-you-from-your-stupor kind of salvo. The first time we heard it, we thought we were dead; the second time we heard it, we realized we were. The third time wiped clean away any concern we had regarding our well-being and we whooped like madmen in our sealed iron tub, hands at the crank, hunched at our stations like crippled industrial workers. Frank yelled like a siren without taking a breath. Augustus hooted like a screech owl. The walls pinged and groaned, but held their seams. We screamed for more.

My name is Ward Lumpkin, and I man the second crank

station aboard the "fish boat" *H. L. Hunley,* the first underwater vessel commissioned for combat by the Confederate States of America. There are seven of us aboard, not including our captain, Lieutenant Dixon, and in navigating the submarine murk of Charleston Harbor we make up the third volunteer crew in as many months. Mechanical failure; flooding ballast tanks; human error; bad luck: conventional wisdom around Battery Marshall has the survival rate aboard the *Hunley* hovering near zero, and that's without ever having engaged an enemy ship. Cannon probability, Augustus calls it, as in, stuff yourself inside a cannon and see what happens. But there's probability, and there's certainty. Antietam was a washout. Gettysburg was worse. Crescent City folded like the house of cards it was and we lost the Mississippi.

And now? In Richmond, war widows have begun rioting over bread. Railways in our control are being blown at such a rate you'd think it was some kind of competition.

One thing, at least, is clear to everyone: the Union naval blockade encircling Charleston must be broken if we are to continue aggression with the North, and if things are ever going to roll our way it'll be by doing the unexpected. General to germ-soaker we fold our hats and stand in awe before the ingenuity of this machine: a cylindrical steam boiler, lengthened and tapered at the ends, outfitted with conning towers, a propeller, and diving fins. Affixed to our bow is a seventeen-foot-long iron spar torpedo that carries 135 pounds of gunpowder, which Frank has taken to calling the Demoralizer. We are the unheard of: an instrument of destruction that maneuvers *under* the waves. If we survive our test dives, if we make it past Breach Inlet without rolling in the tide, if we crank undetected the three miles from the mouth of Charleston Harbor, it's enough ordnance to send any ship we happen to greet to the bottom of the ocean.

"Desperation breeds invention," Arnold has begun saying each time he seals the hatch.

"May wonders never cease," Frank says back.

Arnold Becker, Carleton F. Carlsen, Frank Collins, James Wicks, Augustus Miller, Joseph Ridgaway. Before the *Hunley* arrived in Charleston, before we volunteered our way underwater, all of us were stationed aboard the receiving ship *Indian Chief* off of Battery Marshall. The *Sloop of Invalids,* we called it. The C.S.S. *Not Much to Report.* Everyone aboard had either been shot, trampled, maimed, heavily shelled, amputated, or otherwise shellacked on various campaigns. We suffered from swamp foot, dysentery, low morale, and general incompetence. Our commander, Lieutenant Joosten, enjoyed telling us that he woke each morning wondering about the talents of his crew, and passed each night trying to forget. To a man, we were considered unreliable in combat. Frank had been at Manassas, seen his best friend ribboned by shrapnel, and had dreams like you wouldn't believe. Augustus had stepped on his bayonet while cleaning his rifle and severed a tendon. I was born with a hip irregularity and moved so herky-jerky it made *other* people wince. "Well, I guess we all know why *you're* here," Frank had said when I introduced myself. In response I told a joke about a three-legged plow horse, which either no one heard, or no one got.

On deck, we had an unobstructed view of what Augustus had dubbed our Tableau of Lessening Odds. The Federal blockade was stupefyingly effective. Union canonships patrolled the mouth of the harbor, just out of range, and sank anything we tried to send through with the insouciance of a bull swatting blackflies. At night, they resumed bombardment of the city. High, arching incendiaries, numbering in the thousands, painted the sky. You felt the concussion in your chest.

Damage reports read like the end of the world. Houses, churches, and hotels were demolished. Everything south of Calhoun Street was rubble. Stray dogs ran in packs down the boulevard and looked at whoever was sifting through the wreckage like, *What are* you *doing here?*

On our receiving ship, we sat back, dumbfounded, and familiarized ourselves with new definitions of inadequacy. Supplies were running low. Reinforcements, always coming, never showed. Larger attempts at mobilization had been catastrophic. We practiced knots and evacuation drills, memorized flag signals, and wondered how much longer the city would hold. We'd stand watch, scan the horizon for runners, and return below with a tally of the gulls we'd counted. Downtime was spent staring at cleats.

"I can't say I'm proud of our efforts," Augustus said one day as hundreds of pounds of artillery whistled into Charleston.

"I've addressed the firmament," Frank said back, watching the bombardment with his head in his hands. "And it remains uninterested in your evaluation."

Half our guns had been off-loaded and sent to the front. Those that remained sported the dust of the museum pieces they were. Our defense seemed to consist of getting—and staying—out of range. "If we're not going to actually be *receiving* anything, couldn't we be of more use somewhere else?" Frank said one day to Lieutenant Joosten when he was topside checking inventory.

"Your enthusiasm," Lieutenant Joosten said, looking around as if seeing us for the first time, "is admirable."

After he'd left, Augustus kicked at the rail and broke his toe. Frank counted the picket ships just outside Battery Marshall's cannon line and cursed all fourteen vessels, then our ship, then himself with pleasurable combinations of colorful language. "We're just going to sit here in the pluff mud, watching, until they destroy everything?" Arnold said. "That a rhetorical question?" someone said back.

Two weeks later, on August 12, 1863, the *Hunley* was brought in over rail on a flatcar, transferred to dry dock, and, with the help of thirty-five men and an elaborate pulley system, lowered into the water. We crowded the gunwales. We jostled for a view. The afternoon heat shimmered the air above her like a mirage.

"Cure for what ails you," someone said. "Our secret weapon's an iron pecker."

"For the record," Lieutenant Joosten said, clearing his throat, "that's an underwater iron pecker."

The crowd that had gathered by the dock parted to make room for a group of six nonuniformed men, carrying a long boom with a charge and spar at one end. Even from where I was standing I could see they were less than comfortable handling the load. They attached it gingerly to the bow of the vessel, and backed away.

There were no speeches, no explanations. But who needed one? Just by looking at the thing you knew what it was built for. "You getting emotional?" Frank said.

"I believe I might be," Augustus said. "I believe it may be so."

How unfamiliar are we with what we are capable of? As a child I was Gimpy the Lump Foot, One-Legged Ward, Vomit the Hobbler. The one-room schoolhouse I attended in Columbia was an exercise in controlled explosions. Before school, groups of kids would taunt me until I chased them, then laugh at the shit-show. During school, balled pieces of paper were bounced off the back of my head with Swiss-clock regularity. After school came the fights. My sisters were no help. My father shrugged at my bloody noses and torn shirts and said I had to learn how to stand up for myself sometime. I pointed to my leg. "You know what I mean," he said.

My mother was more sympathetic, taking me, on occasion, in her arms to muffle my sobs. "You have to know your strengths," she said.

As far as I could tell my only strength consisted of taking heroic portions of abuse and folding them into broods so unyielding that no one in my family would approach me for days. I was accused of being inconsolable. I was chastised for my inability to see beyond myself. Sunday sermons exhorted us to forgive and forget, but even then I knew forgiveness was the province of the healthy, of the unbeaten, and that no help was coming. My parents were treated with sympathy for their blessing in disguise. "Pretty good disguise," my father was fond of saying in response.

The *Hunley*'s first crew was gathered from an elite corps of older seamen none of us, until the moment they filed down the dock, had seen before. They threaded through the assembled crowd, accepting slaps on the back from enlisted men. There was a speech at the water by her captain, Lieutenant Payne, of which only fragments of intoned heroism drifted to my ears. Once everyone was below, Lieutenant Payne waved, then saluted and turned to board. After the hatches were sealed we watched the boat for movement and saw no movement. No one cast off. We waited twenty minutes. Finally, the forward hatch opened, and Lieutenant Payne said that while he appreciated our audience, we should return to our duties: the crew was only becoming familiar with instrument placement, and there would be no dive. Eventually they did dive, but the triumph was short-lived. On August 29, as the *Hunley* was out on the water running short surface maneuvers, Lieutenant Payne inadvertently stepped on the lever controlling the diving plane and our fish boat, with her hatches still open, dove, filled with water, and sank. The rescue skiff found Lieutenant Payne treading water amidst a soup of roiling air bubbles, wearing a look so far beyond stricken it resembled paralysis. He was relieved of his command and the *Hunley* was fished from the bottom of the harbor. Five men drowned. She hadn't traveled more than fifty feet from the wharf.

A second crew volunteered, and the boat's inventor, Horace Hunley himself, was brought in from Mobile to assume command. We lined the shore as dive after successful dive was completed. Mud and silt, occasionally churned to the surface by her propeller, marked the vessel's underwater progress. It was like watching a monster patrol a pond. Fifteen minutes; twenty-three minutes; an hour. We bet rations on how long she'd stay down. One day, she ventured only into the shoals, and remained submerged for eighteen minutes. The next, she explored the deepest part of the harbor, stayed under for fifty-seven minutes, and surfaced to applause.

After three weeks of successful practice dives, we waited one afternoon as an excruciating ninety-two submerged minutes ticked by. Augustus paced the gangway. Carleton tied line in and out of Turk's head knots. I scanned the harbor for churn and saw none. We upped our times and doubled our bets in a show of solidarity until finally even we had to concede it was a lost cause. Lieutenant Joosten let us know that word would be sent to General Beauregard: the crew had drowned and a salvage operation would begin in the morning.

Half an hour later, a yell from the harbor sent us topside. "What's the time on that one?" Hunley shouted. He stood half out of the hatch, his clothing soaked, his voice quavering.

It had been two hours and fifteen minutes. The *Hunley* bobbed fifteen feet from the dock like a fishing buoy. We cheered as though we'd won the war.

Augustus had had the highest guess when we stopped betting. "What am I going to do with all this hardtack?" he said, looking at the pile in front of him.

"Rebuild Fort Sumter?" Frank, fanning the heat off his face, said. "Shove it up your ass? Be grateful?"

On October 15, two days before she was scheduled to engage the picket ships, the *Hunley* failed to surface. Three days later, she was found nine fathoms down, her bow augered into the mud, her ballast tanks open and her cabin flooded. The salvage operation confirmed what we already knew: that all eight men, including Horace Hunley, had been trapped aboard, and drowned. The service was brief. We stood at attention, approximated composure, and returned to our ship.

The blockade, as if relieved to have dodged this particular assault, sank two of our runners and shelled a cathedral in celebration.

What kind of person signs up for duty aboard a self-sabotaging vessel that has failed—spectacularly—almost every meaningful test it's been given? Who willingly mans the underwater equivalent of a bicycle strapped to a bomb with the intention of pedaling it four miles through hostile waters to engage an infinitely better equipped enemy? After a two-week hiatus, the *Hunley* was returned to active duty, and her new skipper, Lieutenant Dixon, asked for volunteers. We stepped forward. He was visibly touched. We were touched ourselves. He wondered why, out of over four hundred people, only seven had signed up. We shrugged. He asked if we knew how unlikely a successful mission would be. We nodded. And might he ask why we volunteered.

"You *could*," Frank said, and offered nothing else.

The *Hunley* is thirty-nine feet long with a beam of three feet, ten inches. The entry hatches that cap the conning towers are fourteen by fifteen and a half inches; we swivel our hips diagonally, and even then it's like threading a cannonball through a needle. Below boasts a cabin height of four feet; there is no standing, only sitting. Discomfort, muscle cramps, an iron-smelling darkness; it gets so hot we make jokes about various sins catching up to us in *this* lifetime. Augustus, generally the first below, has taken to greeting us as we crawl past. "The C.S.S. *Steam Boiler* welcomes you aboard," he says.

The seven of us sit on the starboard side, shoulders chafing, hands on the propeller crank. Our legs, if extended, span the beam and come up short on the hull. Lieutenant Dixon perches in the bow, head in the conning tower, levers at the ready. On his signal we turn the propeller. He lights a candle, checks the manometer mounted above his head, and floods the ballast tanks. As we dive, the iron hull sweats and groans like old wood. The air goes from stale to rank. "Yo-ho-ho," someone says.

In August she arrived; in August she sank. In August she rose; in October she sank, only to be salvaged and mobilized again. Every day we board a contraption that has killed thirteen men, including its inventor, on test runs alone. Every night we site the picket ships, set a course, and practice maneuvers. Our purpose is comically straightforward: steer undetected to the mouth of the harbor, sink the largest Union frigate we can ram, hope we are not destroyed in the explosion, and crank ourselves back to shore. To call us brave would imply that we've thought this through. To call us a suicide outfit would be missing the point. How many men have been underwater for hours at a time? How many men have sat crumpled, candlelit, and submerged and been sure of themselves? Frank hums a marching song softly in time with the propeller. Carleton taps the crank handle with his ring finger.

On the hull, rivets have been countersunk to minimize drag. If the tide is with us, if the sea is calm, if we are cranking to absolute capacity, our top speed is four knots. If the water's against us, we have a cruising speed of one knot and are in danger of capsizing. On the rear conning tower Frank's painted "1863" and below it, "Speed Matters Little." Someone else (not one of us) has painted, in smaller letters, "Also: Reason." It shows a basic lack of understanding. As far as we can tell, our Confederacy is on the verge of collapse. What's so unreasonable about wanting to give some of it back?

November and December pass without improvement around Battery Marshall, the focused attention of our war effort shifting from one losing front to another, and enthusiasm regarding our new weapon seems to have tapered from the top down. In the absence of any clear directive, our dives become endurance tests. How deep can we go? How fast can we pump air back into the ballast tanks? We turn tight circles underwater. We set the *Hunley* down on the harbor floor and practice shallow breathing. We dive and surface, acquainting ourselves with immersion. We memorize instrument placement. Attached to the outer hull is extra ballast, iron platelets i-bolted through the floor, which, in case of an emergency, can be unscrewed and dropped. We practice locating them in the dark.

Lieutenant Dixon studies tidal charts. Given that we are hand-powered, whenever we are scheduled to engage the blockade we will need to leave on the ebb tide and return with the flood. We will need the cover of darkness.

"Darkness, darkness, darkness," Frank has taken to saying before Lieutenant Dixon blows out the candle.

"Light, light, light," we say back, once the candle's extinguished. We're fond of the reversal.

There are moments of panic. Episodes of self-doubt that buffet our overall sub-marine elation. We've come to know our time underwater as a dampened and foggy silence punctuated by flashes of distress so immediately visceral it takes us days to stop shaking. During one dive, Lieutenant Dixon forgets to light the candle before setting the diving planes, and accidentally floods the ballast tanks before the rear hatch is fully sealed, taking on enough water that if he hadn't immediately realized his mistake we would've certainly sunk. Another dive, we reverse into a pylon and break the flywheel that houses our propeller. While depth testing, Augustus succumbs to a brief hysteria, and in our rush to surface we almost roll to port. "Pardon that," he says, shaking. He'd almost kicked a hole in the hull. "Pardoned," Frank says.

At the dock we heave ourselves out of the hatch and stretch out flat on our backs, letting the unreality of what we've just done sink in. The men puttering around Battery Marshall shake their heads and keep a distance that signals discomfort. We give them hard looks in return. They've taken to calling us Pickett's Charge, only without the charge. They place bets on the time it will take us to sink ourselves. The odds are on less than a week. We resent the implication. Frank reminds them that the odds haven't changed for the last six weeks running. "So?" one of them says back.

"Whatever happened to patriotism?" Augustus says. "Don't they know war heroes when they see them?"

"Apparently not," Carleton, watching the latest bombardment of Charleston, replies.

One day, following up an idea we had the night before, Augustus rigs a dummy spar and we knock it into the hull of the *Indian Chief*. We're pulled from the water for a week for having a detrimental effect on morale. "So it wasn't the best way to illustrate our potential," Frank says. "But morale? Half of me wishes it'd been a live load."

"Half of you?" someone says back.

Frank and James disappear in a reverie of letter writing. Lieutenant Dixon takes a leave of absence to visit his fiancée. Carleton and I spend the week sitting near the water, throwing pebbles at floating sticks. When Augustus comes back, he tells us our comrades in arms have a new name for the *Hunley:* the peripatetic coffin.

I tell him I like the sound of it. Augustus shrugs. "Incapacitation is as incapacitation does," he says.

"For our parade," Carleton calls over his shoulder to Lieutenant Joosten, who's running an inspection on the torpedo, "how about a full band and seven of South Carolina's finest, untouched beauties?"

"We'll see about a celebration," Lieutenant Joosten, who has a beauty of his own, says, "when you guys actually *do* something."

Our first chance actually to do something comes at the end of December when we receive an order to engage the U.S.S. *Camden,* a sloop of war that has just arrived in the harbor. As we make our preparations, the thump of artillery sounds in the distance. It has also come down from General Beauregard that, for our own safety, we are not to use the *Hunley* as a submersible, but to remain partially surfaced, using the night as camouflage. When this news reaches us, Augustus says nothing. Carleton says nothing. I say nothing.

"Doesn't that defeat the whole purpose of this thing?" Frank says.

"You're looking at me like I have a reassuring answer to that," Lieutenant Dixon says.

We retrieve the torpedo from the armory and carry it the three hundred yards to the dock. My hands are sweating and twice Carleton asks us to stop so he can get a better grip. We fasten the boom to the bow, sit on the dock, and listen to the waves lap the iron sides of the hull. The night is moonless, and very dark.

Without a word, we lower ourselves into the *Hunley*. Infantrymen line the dock wearing expressions caught somewhere between skepticism and disbelief. As we cast off, one of them, a kid wearing a uniform three sizes too big, slowly waves. I close and secure the hatch without waving back.

Lieutenant Dixon sights the *Camden* and calls for a rotational speed of three quarters. He floods the front ballast tank and then gives the signal for Carleton to flood the rear. Beside me, Frank whispers a Hail Mary. Augustus triple checks the i-bolt at his feet. We dive incrementally until only the conning towers are surface-visible and then secure the tanks. Two minutes in, the *Hunley*'s a hothouse. Six minutes in, Lieutenant Dixon blows out the candle, and we're moving in a darkness so complete I feel outside of myself.

It takes us an hour to get to the mouth of the harbor. It takes us another hour to get within half a mile of the *Camden*. Lieutenant Dixon calls for a lower speed, and we're surprised at the sound of his voice. My body's aching from sitting in the same position for so long. My shoulders are on fire. Sweat pools in my boots.

When we're what must be a hundred yards from the ship, Lieutenant Dixon orders us to stop. We take our hands off the propeller, and everything goes silent. We can hear the water breaking in wavelets over the conning towers as we glide forward. We can hear voices, indistinct. Laughter. Shouting. Part of a song. It sounds infinitely far away. For a moment we wonder if we're prepared to do what we came out here for—it seems, suddenly, ungraspable and remote—and then Lieutenant Dixon hisses, "Stop. Reverse."

We do nothing at first. "Reverse," he says again. "It's not the *Camden,* it's just a picket ship."

"What's the difference?" Frank says.

"The difference is that we only have orders to engage the *Camden,*" Lieutenant Dixon says. "Reverse."

"Why don't we just ram it?" I say. "We're out here."

"Reverse."

Because the tide is against us, it takes us four hours to get back. By the time we reach the dock, morning has broken. We sit at our stations, cold with sweat, furious with humiliation. No one wants to get out. Finally Lieutenant Dixon unscrews the hatch. As he heaves himself out, he shakes like he has a palsy. "It wasn't the *Camden,*" he says, to someone at the dock.

"Well, I'll be," the voice comes back.

Opportunities come, opportunities go. We set out to engage the *Hoboken,* but the weather turns us back. We try the next night, but a tiny seam opens in the hull for no apparent reason and we turn back. A week later we get caught in the tide at the mouth of Breach Inlet and are rolled side to side so violently that Frank doesn't eat for two days.

The war drags—slogs—on. On New Year's Day, two runners break the blockade and we're all grins and whoops until their cargo's revealed to be molasses and women's clothing. The ships we try to send through, carrying cotton and rice, are caught by the blockade and send up smoke in dark columns that travel so high before dissipating, the horizon appears jailed. The shelling of Charleston continues unabated, the Federals launching shell after shell into the abandoned city from Morris Island and the harbor as if they have nothing better to do with the afternoon.

To the north of us, General Grant has begun what's promised to be a march of attrition and scorched earth, aimed at Richmond, and we seem unable to muster any sort of resistance. But how could we? We build an iron ship, they build one of theirs. We mobilize for Washington, and they cut us in half in Virginia. We shoot our best general in the back, and even he isn't that surprised about it. "You'd think, standing at a distance," Frank says, "that we're *trying* to lose."

"You'd also think," Carleton, who's sitting next to him, says, "that your emotional response would clock in somewhere above where it apparently is."

Reports place our dead in the tens of thousands. In January, Battery Marshall becomes a way station for casualties. Throughout the night we hear the screams of the newly wounded. Outside the makeshift hospital, amputated legs are stacked like wood until someone complains and they're covered up. "At least now you'll have some company in the hobble department," Augustus says to me. I key my laughter to such a pitch that someone's dog answers from across Battery Marshall and Augustus rapidly excuses himself from the table.

A letter from my mother informs me they've left our property in the face of the advancing Union army, and plan to head east. *What I pray for now,* it reads, *is a swift end to this conflict, so we can be together again.*

I start a letter back and give up halfway through.

During a test dive in February, we spring a leak and the *Hunley* is pulled for repairs. A bolt had come loose, and seawater erupted through the hull in a tiny stream that came up between Carleton's legs in such a way that even Lieutenant Dixon, once safely on the dock, found it amusing. We're told we'll be back in the harbor in four days.

"What's the point?" Carleton says as we secure the torpedo in the armory.

"Of what?" Frank says back.

"Of practice dives? Of *any* of this?"

Frank secures the padlock and turns. He shrugs, palms out, as if checking for rain. "Are you looking for the ontological explanation or something more accessible?" he says, shutting down the conversation.

In the harbor, the picket ships list around their newest arrival: the U.S.S. *Housatonic,* a twelve-cannoned sloop of war that measures over two hundred feet. At twelve hundred tons, she's a thing of fierce beauty. Her appearance is the cause of general concern around Battery Marshall. For us, alone, it's encouraging.

Lieutenant Dixon, for the first time in weeks, visits us in our barracks. He's smaller than I am, and is wearing what Augustus has taken to calling his Look of Officiousness. He stands in the entry, silent, until Frank makes it clear that he should either come out with it or bid us good night. He smiles nervously, fishes in his pocket, and emerges with a twenty-dollar gold piece, dented in the middle.

"My fiancée gave this to me," he begins, and tells his story.

We listen as the thing unfolds. His inaugural morning of combat was at Shiloh, where he was a rifleman in a first-wave offensive blown back so quickly it was held up as a textbook don't in subsequent battles. Bullets whizzed by and lodged in the bodies of the men behind him. The sound of it, he said, was like apples exploding on the side of a barn. Cannon fire shredded his line. As he marched, unsure of himself—standing, so he felt, alone—the gold piece in his pocket caught a musket ball and sent him to the ground. He spent three weeks in the hospital, but kept his leg. "It seems like luck," he says. "But it's not."

He passes it around. It's heavier than I imagined, and gleams in the lamplight. On one side, there's an engraving: *Shiloh April 6 1862 My life Preserver G. E. D.* "Where was this at Vicksburg?" Carleton says, when it's passed to him.

Lieutenant Dixon pockets the gold piece and tugs at his beard. "We engage the *Housatonic,*" he says. "As soon as we're repaired." He turns and leaves.

"As long as this is inspirational story hour," Arnold says

from his bunk and cuts wind. Coincidence, pluck, promises, talismans—what does any of that have to do with us? We know what we see and what we've always seen: a campaign of indiscriminate shelling, economic paralysis, and relentless destruction. The strategy of the more powerful and better equipped. The Union giant's footsteps thundered down our hallway the instant we struck our flints on Fort Sumter, and their response has so far outstripped the ethereal bonds of brotherhood that we blanch at our capacity for self-regard. How will we explain that we brought this on ourselves? How do you meet, halfway, a hammer blow that's larger than anything you can imagine? And how long can you do nothing before you begin to feel you deserve it?

Frank takes one of Arnold's boots and pulls the laces clean off. Arnold puts up his fists and Frank apologizes. "It was my intention," he says, "to unlace both."

"Intentions, intentions," Augustus says. "Never the follow-through."

Frank shrugs. He leans over, finds Arnold's other boot, yanks the laces, and ties the boot closed. We have our fish boat. We have our bomb. We possess what the less observant might call an indifference to plausibility, which is matched only by our private desire to transfer this thing back to a human scale. We have what Augustus calls our Stab at Enlargement. Everything else hovers in a constant state somewhere just beyond recognition.

Before going to sleep, Carleton convinces Augustus to tell his balloon corps story. It's one of our favorites; we know it by heart. Before stepping on his bayonet, Augustus had fought in Virginia with General Beauregard. Things hadn't been going well. They were being outmaneuvered: any flank operation they attempted was spotted far ahead of time by the Union Balloon Corps—lookout men in balloons, who surveyed the land from the air and reported on Confederate flanking formations. These balloons were something to see. They hung in the sky like inverted onion bulbs, tethered to the ground. You kept waiting for them to sprout. They'd been bad news for the last few months, spotting and shucking any surprises General Beauregard could dream up. One night, the night before a planned mobilization, Augustus's commander recruited a small group of soldiers and tasked them with a covert, and potentially dangerous, operation: they were to leave their encampment, bushwhack across the Union lines, fire on the corps, and return. No one in the balloons would be armed, and, if they managed their surprise, there would be minimal protection on the ground. Augustus and four other soldiers were given three muskets each, grimly saluted, and sent on their way. They ran like Indians through the forest, ducking branches, kneeling in the brush. It took them two hours to get within range, and another hour of crawling on their stomachs to get a clear view of the balloons. Afraid of being seen, they were quick to load and arrange their extra muskets in a row on the grass in front of them. At one of their whispered commands, they shouldered for the first volley. As Augustus lined and steadied his shot, he caught a glimpse of the man in the basket. He was small and bespectacled. He looked completely at peace.

It took two volleys to puncture the balloon. Beset by a sudden bolt of conscience—what Augustus calls one of his finer moments of not connecting the dots—he'd been very careful to aim well above the bespectacled man on his second shot. The basket fell. The man plummeted in silence and hit a patch of rocks. The sound was like a melon breaking. The musket reports brought the Union soldiers out of their tents, but by the time they figured out what had happened, Augustus was streaking back to camp, musket-less and exhilarated by the sound of panicked Union guns firing at the copse of trees where they had just been.

Confident he'd dismantled the enemy's ability to under-cut his formations, General Beauregard drafted his plans and slept the sleep of the satisfied.

The next day thousands of men—including Augustus's commander and all four of the men who'd accompanied him through the forest the night before—died.

"Turns out," Augustus says, "balloons weren't the problem."

We are quiet for a few minutes. Then Frank breaks the silence by telling Augustus he never tires of that particular story.

"I do," Augustus replies, and turns his back to the rest of us to sleep.

Two nights later, the repairs have been made. We make our way to the wharf and run a quick inspection, our fish boat patient and quiet as we check the outside of her hull, crouch to run our hands across her deck, dip our fingers in the water. We secure the torpedo with care, triple-checking the firing mechanism. Lieutenant Dixon is in full regalia, his pistols crossed below his bandolier. The tassels of his shoulder ensigns sweep with his movement like grass in the wind. A gibbous moon hangs suspended over Breach Inlet, mirror-reflected in the water. We lower ourselves into the *Hunley* barely aware of one another. No one sees us off. As we go hands on the propeller and prepare to flood the ballast tanks, Carleton remarks on the thorough pleasantness of this February evening. It hadn't occurred to any of us that the shelling had stopped.

The *Housatonic* sits two and a half miles outside of Battery Marshall, sails reefed, becalmed. On Lieutenant Dixon's orders, we crank slowly, a partially submerged monster of complete silence.

We leave the inlet and churn at our stations for what could be one hour or five, lost in the rhythm of our cranking. We know we are closing the distance; we care about nothing else. Fifty yards from the ship, Lieutenant Dixon calls for maximum speed and we oblige. Thirty-five yards away we are spotted and some sort of bell aboard the *Housatonic* peals alarm. We are too close for their cannons, but musket balls fired from deck ricochet off our conning towers—the only part of the *Hunley* they can see—and the sharp pings of impact are amplified between us, marbles tossed against a heavy iron tub. There is shouting, and I'm not sure if it's coming from us or somewhere else.

The hollow thunk of our spar as it embeds itself in the

wooden hull of the *Housatonic* jolts us forward; we scramble to regain our positions. Lieutenant Dixon yells for reverse. It takes us a second to remember which direction to crank until Frank says "Away from you" and we put it together. I'm aware that we're moving at an angle, our stern dipping low, leading the bow below the surface. We glide in reverse for just long enough to wonder whether we've attached the line to the firing mechanism correctly, and then there's an explosion so deafening it's like tasting sound.

We take our hands off the crank and stare at the iron wall two feet in front of us. I can feel an arm on my shoulder, applying pressure. I'm vaguely aware of a hand on my leg. My feet are cold.

Lieutenant Dixon lights his candle and swivels in his seat. His expression is unreadable. He asks Carleton to check the ballast tank. He tells Frank to re-secure the rear hatch. When they tell him all is as expected, three quarters full, secured, he closes his eyes and lets his chin fall to his chest. I look down. We're sitting shin-deep in water.

Battery Marshall is two and a half miles away. No one says anything. The swell bobs us back and forth, gently sloshing the water we've taken on, now at our knees, as if in a basin. Lieutenant Dixon tells us that through the porthole he can see the *Housatonic* in flames, listing to port. Lifeboats are being lowered. Men are in the water. We remain at our stations as he unscrews the front hatch and fires a magnesium flare, signaling success. Then he secures the hatch and returns to his seat without a word.

The *Hunley* fills fast. We stop moving in the swell, and I have the sensation of diving without diving. When the water's at my waist, I wonder if we'll make it to the bottom of the harbor before we drown. I imagine a gentle cessation, silt and mud pillowing out and up, then settling. I imagine rust and barnacles, inquisitive fish. When the water's at chest level, Frank mumbles something and puts his head under. No one restrains him.

When the water's at my neck, my father appears. He asks me if I know that, one hundred years from now, the *Hunley* will be found and fished out of the harbor by an expedition costing millions of dollars, and, once salvaged, will be paraded through the streets of Charleston by young men dressed in gray uniforms. He asks me if I know that they'll find a boot and a button, and verify that Arnold had been one of the men aboard. That, eventually, they will find Lieutenant Dixon's gold coin, dented in the middle, and a great effort will go into finding out what happened to his fiancée—whose name, it turns out, was Queenie—but that her story will prove mysterious, no beginning, just an ending, as it is with us. He asks me if I know that, despite sustaining over seven million pounds of artillery, Charleston will never succumb to Union occupation.

"Did you," he says, "ever wonder at this?"

I tell him that at every turn our understanding of what was happening around us had been mitigated by such a clanging abashment that we'd become rock-like as far as expectations go. It was pick-up sticks in the middle of a hurricane. It had never occurred to us to wonder about much of anything.

He tells me that we will be remembered mostly for our optimism. I tell him it isn't optimism that gets you aboard something like this. He says, Still.

I ask him what we've done beyond proving our own uselessness? What are we but a spectacle of self-defeat? He answers that we are an expression of an intangible truth that has plagued victors for thousands of years. That immolation as a form of confrontation holds irreducible power.

I tell him he has it backward, and if it had been approval we were looking for, we would've kept diaries.

There is another explosion above us, the keel of the *Housatonic* seizing in on itself, collapsing, and my father disappears. Through the darkness I feel the iron hull on my back. I feel for the crank handle and grasp it. Carleton is frantic. Augustus is standing so his head is in the small hollow of the conning tower, which will be the last place to fill. Someone is screaming at a pitch both familiar and thoroughly distant, a keening that only stops, and briefly, in surprise when our stern hits the floor of the harbor and our bow follows, scrapes a rock of some kind, and rests.

summer boys

Friends, two boys, stare at each other and themselves in the slightly warped mirror in the second-floor bathroom of a small house in Laurelhurst, shorts on, shirts off. It's the summer after fifth grade, and school, for them, is already beginning to seem like a dream that belongs to someone else. It's in their slipstream. Gone. The days are beginning to get *hot* hot, there's a Popsicle man somewhere, but right now? They don't care. They're almost exactly the same age—their birthdays are four days apart, a cosmic near-miss that in their calculations brings them just short of being brothers, twins, the way things were supposed to be. One of them, the older-by-four-days friend has a younger sister; the other only parents, and, standing next to his friend, in his friend's house, he feels a deformity calmed. Their chests are concave; their feet are growing. Their arms are marbled with the musculature of tiny woodland creatures. One has an innie, the other an outie. No one is home.

One of them, the taller one, holds a hair clipper that belongs to his father, a clipper that has been rescued from the dank recesses of an upstairs closet in the Laurelhurst house, a closet that smells like soap and shoes and motor oil and is as dark as dark gets, and he is saying to the other that now is the time to do this; now, while his father's at work in the motorcycle garage where he's employed on Saturdays; now, while his mother is at the market getting groceries that will include, per the boys' special request, Fruity Pebbles, Gushers, Dr Pepper, and frozen pizza (which is the reason they are always at this house; the other house is nothing but wheat germ and raisins, wooden cars and make-your-own-fun, early bedtime and no TV, ever); *now* is the time, he says, now is the *time*. It is 1987, and Brian Bosworth, the terror from Oklahoma, has arrived in Seattle to play for the Seahawks; it's time to make the magic happen. They love Walter Payton, they love Jim McMahon, they love the Bears (mostly because one of the boys' fathers, the father they idolize, loves the Bears), but it's more accurate to say they loved, because now the Boz is here, a hometown hero, an eleven-million-dollar man who will unify the city and bring a form of gilded greatness to the Northwest, and his arrival has obliterated everything else in their orbit of likes and dislikes.

Think of the Boz, the boy holding the clipper says. The haircut was his idea. *Think* of the *Boz,* he says again, as if they were capable, at this moment, of thinking about anything else. He's theirs now. The Boz, picked in the supplemental draft, belongs to them. He has hair from the future, spiked on top, bare on the sides, and in back a flowing river of awesomeness that sneaks out from under his helmet. The Boz wears his torn jersey *outside* his pants. The Boz marks his ankle-tape with his college number, 44, because the NFL won't allow that to be his official number, which is 55—an echo, certainly, but a pale one. The switch is flipped; the clipper's mosquito hum fills the second floor. This will not be just any haircut. This will be *the* haircut, and with it they will become part of something bigger than themselves. This, one of them thinks, is a pivotal moment. It's a jumbotron experience, a statistical miracle, and they are doing it together. It's not about being like someone. It's about becoming him. And with a few swipes and a scalp reveal you can *make* it happen. They are tender, precise with each other. They take turns. Concentrate on the line. Hair falls to the tile, dirty snow-clumps on the bathroom floor.

Do they look like the Boz, with their torn jerseys and markered-up shoes? Do they look like the Boz, when they have brown hair and he's decidedly platinum? Does anyone care? Before this, they were just friends, certain of their affection, uncertain of its expression. Before this, one of them, the worrier, was afraid that his hours in the Laurelhurst house were numbered, that he would overstay his welcome, that he would be exposed as an interloper, but that worry is now gone. The haircut is proof. The haircut is a leveler. So do they look like the Boz, who could curl their combined weight without so much as a lip-twitch? Who cares! They look like each other, and that, for one of them, is good enough.

Their hair clogs in the sink; they leave it there. Hair, impossible, at this point, to say whose, is on the counter; they leave it there. Hair, little splinters of it, covers every bathroom surface, including, somehow, the mirror, and they, the two of them, are down the stairs like future linebackers, swinging their weight around the shoddy banister, obliterating the weak side run. The grandfather chair on the first floor becomes Bo Jackson. The screen door is the Broncos porous offensive line. Outside the sun is high, and the front yard is the Kingdome. Plays are called, random numbers, slow huts, sharp hikes, and the trees lining the street, the great oaks and elms that have been watching over this particular block for who knows how long, who have seen how many plays called, how many errant, throwing-starred punts go up on the roof, who hold, in their branches, a generation's worth of Aerobies too high to knock out—these trees, who have enjoyed, for centuries it seems, those magical on-the-lawn hours when balls are drawn heavenward, who have stood in rapt attention for those endless minutes before the car-door-slamming parents return from the outside world to ask their kids what the hell, just what the hell is going *on*, these trees, they whistle their applause.

Stop rubbing your dicks together, says the boy's father when he gets back from the garage and sees their hair, *he's not that great*. They are sitting at the dinner table, he has just pulled up a chair, and his voice is like the phlegmatic roar of a garbage disposal. Each word a lifetime of cigarettes. One of the boys is used to the sound of this voice. The other is not, but wishes, *thinks,* he could be. The two of them take all criticism delivered from the mouth of this man seriously, this man who rides motorcycles and has promised to teach them, soon, to ride, this man who carries in his limbs the promise of casual violence and who wears a look of weary surprise upon entering the rooms of his own house as if he can't quite believe what his life has handed him, this man, they are attuned to him—but this time one of them can't take what he's said seriously, because he's just heard the word *dick* said aloud. Inside! In the presence of a mother who doesn't bat an eyelash as she slaps the molten pizza on the table. To his relief, he sees his friend is already laughing. Words like this send the two of them into hysterical revelry. *Butt, crack, nuts, ballpeen,* these words are everywhere, and they're hilarious. A family history of angina, the recent and casual mention of it, was close enough to the real thing that the one boy's mother told them to go ahead and get it out of their system and then knock it off. The father's more indulgent, telling them now through monstrous bites of pizza that their one and only Brian Bosworth received the Dick Butkus award not just once but twice, and try saying that five times fast. They try, of course they try, and the effort almost brings them off their chairs. Later this father buys his son a Land of Boz poster to replace their now unloved and forgotten Jim McMahon on his bedroom wall. Their tank-topped hero: wide-stanced, implacable, and domineering in wraparound shades. Across his chest it reads "Monster D.B. 44"—*defensive back,* the father explains—and he's flanked by menacing kids their own age wearing shades, a menacing Tin Man, a stepped-on Scarecrow, and a Dorothy pinup who has laced her small arm around his just so, in that perfect way. It's an invitation that for now does nothing for the two boys, not just yet, because directly below where she has placed her hand in the crook of his elbow the Boz is palming a football helmet, his fingers dug in, the helmet an egg, the helmet not going anywhere. The father hadn't been leveling criticism, judgment, at all, the boys understand. It's just the way men talk to each other. The friends stare at the poster for hours, and imagine that instead of there being only one Boz standing guard at the foot of a road that leads, behind him, to a spired and mysterious Emerald City, there are two.

Weeks pass and here's how the boys talk to each other: What do you like? What do you like? Is that something we should like? Every day is a disputation of taste, and nothing ascends without the explicit approval of both. When they wrestle, one wins. The next time they wrestle, the other wins. Some things they can do nothing about (chins, eye color, hand size); others (shoes, hair, room decoration, lunch box) they can. For one of the boys, the unworried one, this equilibrium seems a natural, effortless state; for the other, it's become everything. What do you like? I like what you like. Up in one of the trees in the yard, on a climbable but out-of-the-way branch, they've carved their first names followed by a last name they made up.

These friends, two boys, they spend their days—all their days it seems, the one boy's mother wondering what's wrong with *this* house—in Laurelhurst, going to the beach, swimming, jumping off the high platform, mugging for each other on the way down, playing rag-tag in the water with a sock-covered tennis ball they peg at each other like Norwegian berserkers. They get splinters from running on the old dock, wooden shards they extract, painfully, with the mother's tweezers. They roll the log-boom for hours, so good at it that eventually their suits actually dry in the sun. They scrape their elbows on cement, they hyperextend on trampolines, they tear their baseball pants sliding in the rec-field diamonds, wounds that weep clear liquid and require rubbing alcohol. They mis-time their tree-climbing dismounts and roll their ankles, they play butt-ball off the garage door until their backs are patterned with bruises, swing pillows like merciless cudgels, chuck super-bounce balls into traffic from the cover of shrubs. Their days are long and they are war buddies, forging experience. Long days, and enough time to explore the texture of friendly violence without consequence until one of the boys, while running, kicks playfully at the other's back foot and sends him sprawling. An accident, an accident, he wants to shout even before his friend hits the ground, his arms so surprised by the physics of what is happening to him that they don't even consider reaching down to break the fall. Accident, as one of the boys lands hard on his face, scrapes the bridge of his nose, blackens his eye, and screams like a bird of prey until his mother hustles from the kitchen to hold him in her arms; the other, unhurt, standing, guilty, numb, listening, is surprised to find himself wishing not that it hadn't happened, but that it had happened, instead, to him. Back in the kitchen, he hands his friend an ice pack, and then takes one for himself; he puts it on his own uninjured face, and pushes it into his eye until it hurts the back of his head, says, *oh, shit, ow,* a thing so dumb to do, an action so transparent, that everyone at the table laughs. All is forgiven. It was a mistake. He will not be sent home. The pain subsides.

The next morning, in the garage, they trick their bikes out with Spokey Dokes and then pedal out into the neighborhood, jumping curbs, careening down stairs, and calling out their favorite parts of their new favorite movie, *Rad,* which is about BMX bike racers who jump over things larger than curbs until Jeremy, an older cousin, released to his own summer and suddenly present, tells them bike riding's for faggots, since *bike* is German for *dick,* and so then what are you doing when you ride your bike? Neither of the boys are German, this is information they hadn't known. Jeremy, and his rumbling skateboard, here to deliver the news. They are open to it, to this attention from Jeremy; or, at least, are interested enough to hear what he has to say. He's about to enter high school. He's got hair that is not buzzed, but ratty and long. Though he lives only a few blocks over he's never once expressed even a passing interest in either of them; they are eager to prolong this exchange, and even feel, on this day, strangely blessed by it. They watch him kick-flip his skateboard. They watch his loping leg-push, and his deep lean as he carves back toward them, kicks again, and stops a few feet away. What's wrong with your *eye*? Jeremy says. What's wrong with your *hair*? What, he says, is with the matching sweatshirts?

They are caught off guard by the certainty of this questioning. They stand silently astride their bikes, one boy waiting for the other to speak up, not daring to defend the two of them himself. Jeremy is not his cousin. But his friend does not speak up, and the worry returns. Have they been wrong this whole time? Is their closeness being called into question? The thought hovers, takes hold, then disperses as Jeremy kick-pushes lazily down the street, back to his house. Hey, rich boy, he calls over his shoulder. Can you do this? Try copying this. The skateboard flips under his feet, once, twice, catching the sun like an airborne, twisting fish, and then is pulled out of its orbit and expertly stomped to the concrete by Jeremy's mismatched Converse high-tops. I'm not rich, one of the boys says to the other when Jeremy is out of sight. It's not a bad thing, the other says back. As they walk their bikes home, one of the boys runs his fingers through his hair. The Boz, somewhere, looks out disapprovingly at the prospect of his short career.

Soon bikes are out, Spokey Dokes are out, BMX movies are out, Velcro crotch guards are out, wheel-pegs are out, and skateboards are in. It's not only Jeremy telling them this. They've just seen *Back to the Future* on VHS, where Michael J. Fox goes back in time and *invents* the skateboard, which he then rides while holding on to the back of a car. All information received from the movies they watch is stored and internalized and mulled over until it reemerges as want and necessity. How come we didn't see this earlier? one of them says. The back of a *car*! the other says back. They beg for the same skateboard, a Nightmare III model available only at one store, a store that happens to be near the motorcycle garage. This is the model Jeremy has.

When the skateboards are delivered they plaster them with Garbage Pail Kids and spend hours on their butts, lugging down hills, braking with their heels—*burning heel rubber,* they call it—trudging back up to do it again. They carve great slalom curves in the asphalt, bracing themselves against the sound of the wheels on the concrete and the streaming wind. They are doing this for themselves, for the joy in it, for the concrete-streaking pleasure of it all, but who are they kidding? They want an audience, and at the bottom of every hill, they are looking for Jeremy. He is becoming part of their summer. In the driveway, they spend a weekend trying to unlock the secret of the ollie, which Jeremy can do but won't explain, opting instead to rub his knowledge in their faces by ollie-ing anything available—curbs, footballs, tipped over garbage cans. One of the boys, the one who is related to Jeremy, watches Jeremy kick his board, sail over a patch of grass, and land in the street, and tells him that, for *that* maneuver, he gets the Dick Butkus Award. Jeremy eyeballs the two friends, sitting on their own useless skateboards, and says, that better be a *good* thing. They assure him it is. He's three years older, and they want to love him the way they love each other, they want that to be allowed; they want him to love them, to need them, to show them everything he knows about everything because surely,

surely, he knows. All Jeremy wants to talk about, though, are boners and how many girls he's fingered, and how he's going to bag-tag a pinup someday, just like the Boz, in that faggoty poster, hanging above the bed.

Jeremy, called home, ollies a football in the driveway, leaving in his wake a vapor trail of effortless superiority. The friends feel a relief in being alone again, or, at least, one of them does—unobserved, by themselves on their skateboards as the dimmer switch on the day is gradually lowered—but there's also a new feeling of absence that bombards them atomically, nickels of doubt streaming invisibly sideways like a radio frequency. The sun is down, the streetlamps flicker on. But it is only the middle of summer, and an ocean of days stretches in front of them like an endless and gently whispered invitation, and they return to their hill to luge, strobe-lit, through the neighborhood.

These are their moments of gathering. At the house in Laurelhurst, in the June heated nights, in the July afternoons, down in the basement where it just feels like night and a Ms. Pac-Man arcade game stands in the corner unmoving like a dim-lighted guardian, they give in with slack-jawed fervor to the movies they're allowed to rent: *Ghostbusters, Pee-wee's Big Adventure, Gremlins, Lost Boys, Goonies, Flight of the Navigator, White Fang, Explorers.* Is there anything they won't watch? They repeat dialogue and collapse, laughing, into the wide recess of the L-shaped couch, the couch they eat on, the couch they spill soda on, the couch they fort up, the couch they sleep on, in their matching sleeping bags, heads almost touching so that even after it comes from upstairs that it's time, finally, to *shut up* and *turn in*, they can still whisper those moments in the movie they'll see again, in the morning, before it's due at the video store. They're building a common store of references; they're building a language. Before *Godzilla 1985*, they watch a cartoon they cannot get enough of; it's part of the movie, leading in on the VHS tape, a short animated feature called *Bambi Meets Godzilla*. It's a minute long, maybe less. Bambi, munching grass, minding her business, stands in a field. Then, without warning, a gigantic, green, dinosaur-scaled foot *cavooms* down from the top of the screen. Crunch. No more Bambi. Afterward, the Godzilla foot wiggles its claws, as if to say, what can you do?

They rewind it, and watch it again. They rewind it, and show it to Jeremy.

They watch him the way they watch each other, trying to gauge his response, eager to see the laughter on his face the moment before it breaks. He loves it. The two friends, these boys, don't think they've ever been so happy. I've got a movie, he says, after they've rewound and watched it three or four times. I've got a movie. Give me five dollars, and I'll bring it over tomorrow. The friends look at each other. I know you have five dollars, Jeremy says to one of the boys. It'll blow your mind. The money is handed over. Their minds are already blown.

But Jeremy doesn't show up, tomorrow or the next day.

Is he on vacation? they wonder aloud. Does he have summer school? Does he have other friends? They have his phone number, or at least, his parents' phone number—they found it in the emergency book near the phone—but can't bring themselves to call because they have no idea what they'd say. Weeks are passed in the driveway, kicking skateboards back and forth. These friends, the two young boys, are crestfallen at the rejection, and not even the Boz, not even butt-ball, not even the Ghostbusters, not even the release of a new edition of Garbage Pail Kids can mitigate the heartbreak, the disappointment, the fundamental *lameness* they feel. They sit on their skateboards for hours at a time, unmoving. One of them senses the end of something approaching, and waits desperately for the feeling to dissipate. The other seems uninterested in rescuing himself. What do you want to do? Nothing. I want to do nothing. Movies? Skateboards? Ms. Pac-Man? No. Bikes? one of them says, and regrets it immediately. What's wrong with *you* guys? the mother asks at breakfast. Cereal is stirred into chocolate milk mush. The day holds no promise. We suck, one of the boys says. Don't say *suck*, his mother says back. She turns to the other boy. Doesn't your mother miss you?

She does. They separate. Back in his own familial orbit, three miles away in a house that is larger but contains no motorcycles, no pizza, no Boz poster, no television even, one of the boys feels hollowed-out, cheated. He's been cleaved from his brother, from his almost-twin, from what he considers a better version of himself. At night, he lies on his bed, staring at old, night-glow constellations, stickers stuck permanently on his ceiling, which embarrass him now, and imagines every-thing he's missing. His friend hasn't called. And for reasons he can't quite articulate but have to do with wanting to be wanted, with needing equilibrium, the new fear that maybe, just maybe, he will say the wrong thing, he doesn't call his friend. And with every hour that passes, the distance between them begins to feel like space distance; within days, they are galaxies apart. By himself, he organizes his Garbage Pail Kids and his Seahawk trading cards. By himself in the bathroom, he examines the flash lines cut in his hair, now growing in, his body recovering itself. By himself, he becomes a storm-system of self-doubt, unsure of anything except that wherever he is, he is not where he needs to be. His father draws up a list of chores that need to be done if he's just going to spend the rest of his summer sulking inside, so he goes outside and plays butt-ball for hours against his own garage, refusing to have any fun at all, relishing the picture of dejection he's painting for anyone and everyone watching. The tennis ball bounces off the garage door and gets past him, rolling for half a block before disappearing down a rain gutter. This, the boy feels, is about as unendurable as anything he's ever experienced. *What am I missing?* he thinks. *What is it?* His mother, a woman so kind that even he knows it, asks him why he doesn't go down a few blocks, and see what Charles Todds, the son of her friend, is up to. Because, he says, Charles is a fag. And a rich dork. And fat. His mother stares at him in disbelief, and looks like she might cry. *And because,* he wants to add, but doesn't, be-cause his mom is already laying into him about the importance of kindness, *Charles doesn't know anything about me*. His dad walks into the kitchen holding a sleeping bag, playing a hunch, and sees the boy and his mother locked in some sort of silent push-pull, and, because he is unsure of what, just what in the world has happened, he hoists the stuffed sack aloft like he's trying to keep it dry while wading through a river. How about some camping? he says. It's camping season. How does that sound? The boy knows he doesn't have much of a choice in the matter. Camping it is.

Sticks, rocks, heat, dust, bugs. His parents insist on parking the car and hiking to a campground, where it's less likely they'll run into any beer drinkers or loud partyers, and after what feels like hours of death-marching they finally stop, in the middle of the woods, and pitch their REI family-size tent. They do, in fact, see no one else for three days. The days, unpunctuated, feel like weeks to the boy. What is he supposed to do, he thinks, stare at banana slugs all day? Climb a tree? His parents are happy reading, reveling in the isolation after having given up asking him *what's wrong, what's wrong with you these days?* The boy takes his army knife and saws branches into kindling for hours. He knows, with a certain sadness that manifests as anger, and feels like some sort of accelerated aging, that he'd do anything, *anything,* to get back to the house in Laurelhurst. Finally they pack it in. When he gets home, there's a message on the machine from his friend, wondering if, when he comes back, he could come over. The boy is elated.

His mother drops him off. His friend is upstairs, in his

bedroom, sitting cross-legged on the floor, and when he stands with a *hey* there's a mutual feeling of relief, of rightness, of completion, like a reflection meeting its source. It's like that. But also, it's not like that? The Land of Boz poster has been taken down. His friend's haircut has been normalized. There is, at first, a strange formality to their interaction, as if years, rather than weeks, have passed. One of the boys looks at the other like a question mark, noticing his friend has closed a little, his face slightly different than he remembers, as if, in their time apart, his memory has played a small trick on him. This feeling hovers, just beyond recognition but threatening to take hold, until one of them tentatively unloads his pockets to produce three packs of unopened Garbage Pail Kids and then the uncertainty lifts the way it's always lifted. It's the middle of August, and the hot summer days are coming to a shimmering close, but there's still time, now, to skateboard down the street, still time to rent a video, still time to call plays in the front yard, and cut matching streak lines in their hair with the closet clippers if that's what it'll take to erase whatever it is that has come between them. These two friends, they will never need anyone else. The gulf will be bridged. That's what friends are, that's what friends can do. They will be college roommates, twin terrors on the football field, playing not only defensive tackle but iron-manning it, switching off quarterback and wide-receiver duty, playing safety. Whatever this is, one of the friends thinks, there is time to figure it out. There is time to fix it. There is a lag-time between them now, though, a circuit delay, as if they have run two cans together with string and insist on speaking through those even though they are standing four feet apart. One of the boys wants to say to the other, what *happened*, you are not *you* (by which he means, you are not me), but can't find the words to say it, and in fact thinks that maybe his friend knows something he doesn't, and it's this thought that he must put from his head.

Do the parents notice this? Do parents notice anything? Would they turn their head even if a planet, on a collision course, appeared suddenly above? Food is procured. *Godzilla 1985* is rented, the clerk, who is Jeremy's age, giving them the eyebrows, like, *again?* Down into the cool basement, the cassette is slipped into the player. The cartoon, the opening credits, the enormous man-lizard sweeping fire across the city, the fleeing Japanese hordes. The voices are dubbed, and the words don't match the shape of the mouth that is making them, the emotional inflection one assumes was originally there in the performance turned up to a flat yell. And it is when the atomically awakened monster is wading back into the Japanese sea that one friend turns to the other and says that Jeremy had been over, and he had brought his movie, and they had watched it while his parents were gone.

A feeling of complete desolation washes over one of the boys. In his mouth, he tastes, jealously, the tang of exclusion, the finality of the reveal. He feels this way because, secretly, he always knew this would happen. Jeremy isn't his cousin. This is not his house, after all. His father doesn't talk like a cigarette dispenser. His mother doesn't take him on junk food supermarket sweeps. It was never his poster to pin up and take down. He's *always* been a visitor, a home-peeper—a pervert frosting the glass. He's known it without knowing it, and now he feels exposed. They are lying, the two of them, on the L-shaped couch. In the corner, Ms. Pac-Man silently, automatically, perpetually munches pixels. Without me? the boy wants to shout. You did that without me? But he doesn't shout, because he doesn't know how to shout at his friend. He doesn't know, even if he wants to. What he wants is fifth grade again. What he wants is June. What he wants is matching BMX bikes. The basement is suddenly cold, the television now playing a blue screen that bathes everything in the room in an aquarium murk. Maybe he should be shouting at himself.

But he looks at his friend, who has stood up to walk across the carpet to the television. He looks at his friend, who is wearing sweatpants markered with the number 44. He watches as his friend pulls, from the video case for *Back to the Future,* a new video, which is not *Back to the Future,* slips it into the VHS machine, and turns the sound on the television all the way down. He watches as the movie begins, and his throat catches, and he looks at his friend, who is sitting cross-legged in front of the screen, not three feet away from the television, like he's done this before. Both of them know what they are watching, neither of them know whether they should be watching it. You have to get close, one says to the other. The tang of jealousy disappears, and is replaced by something else. They watch the screen, unhearing, until one of them turns the volume up two bars, and the sound fills the basement. They know they are supposed to like this, they know they should be popping boners, readjusting their pants; they know they should be thrilled by what they are seeing, that it should drive them out of their minds, that they should want to see the whole movie but this is happening for neither of them. They are just boys. It's been a summer of black eyes, of scabbed knees, of haircuts, and now it's the summer neither of them are sure they're ready for, the summer that comes from the television, a summer that feels like overreaching. Each feels the sensation of swimming alone for the first time, each feels the orbital pull of planet-collision. It's Jeremy's video. Do you want me to go first, or do you want to go first, one of the friends, the boy who lives in the house in Laurelhurst, says to the other.

What is it like? I don't know. Did you like it? I don't know. Was it bad? It was weird. Why are you crying? I'm not crying. Did he like it? He said he did, one of them says. He said it's what you do. One of them says. One of them. Always.

Upstairs, there are parents. Three miles away, there are parents. And the sound of all of this, it carries. Through the floorboards, through the chimney, through the branches of the guardian trees, up toward the dimming sky. The motorcycle man, the three-pack-a-dayer, who is sitting upstairs with his wife, watching television in the darkened living room, and who, perhaps, has been drinking, has a feeling he can't identify and doesn't question. He stands. Checks the doors to make sure they're locked. Turns on the front light. Walks down the hall, and opens the basement door quietly, soft enough not to wake anyone sleeping, cracked enough to hear if there's any sort of structural damage being done by the two boys in the basement. He opens the door, is about to yell down to them that it's time to knock it off and turn in, and stops. Something trips a wire in the back of his head: a sound, a feeling, he isn't sure. He is a picture, now, of fatherly concern. He is ready to be angry. He places one heavy, slippered foot on the first basement step. A second step follows.

But these friends, what do they hear? Not the movie, playing behind them. Not a father, coming down the stairs. They are hearing nothing but each other. There are no words, but they are talking, now, in the language of friends, in the language of the basement, in the language of hapless Japanese commuters aboard a miniature subway car that has, to their surprise, been picked up by a disinterested, atomic aberration and held high over a Tokyo street. It is, they would admit to each other if they could, thrilling to be left so alone. One friend is clumsily showing the other—the other, who knows nothing of himself, except that he wants to be included, and to show his gratitude that he has been. There is milky, hairless skin. There is the L-shaped couch, dominating the room, and the idea, for one of them, of an ice pack plunged deep into an orbital socket. There is a flaccid taste, the bending of limbs, and a strange, tongue-less kiss. It's a time-out. It is outside of time. They've whistled themselves to the bench, to regroup, tenderly, before suiting up again, and for now, it is just the two of them in this room. The doors are shut. No one is allowed in. It's the end of summer, and they are looking, again, for that old equilibrium, attempting to make sense out of nonsense, and it comes out physically, robotically, without inflection, and it needs to be dubbed. The question that one friend is asking the other is, Where were you? Where were you when this was happening to me? And the answer, a fractured, proffered gift, is the first lie one has ever told the other, though it will take him years to figure that out. The answer is: Right here. I was in this basement, where I belong. I was always in this basement, and I will be in this basement the rest of my life, if that's what you need from me.

john,
for christmas

On the radio, they were calling it "snow-mageddon." Joan had seen the storm on the news, as well, in a Doppler-radar swirl pulsing like a sick heart over the Cascade Mountains. The worst of it was supposed to hit tomorrow, midday, but already the snow had begun to fall in little eiderdown flakes, salting the bushes, promising cover. Her husband, Thomas, was upstairs. Earlier this morning he'd called weather prediction an inexact science. It comes, it goes, one never knows, he'd said. A little song. But this particular storm couldn't arrive early. John—their son, the actor, the writer, the destructively depressed, self-proclaimed failure—was coming home for Christmas, driving up from Oregon with his girlfriend, and the thought of them stuck somewhere, the car they'd bought for him wedged in a snowdrift like a blunt splinter . . . It'd be on the evening news: the only people to freeze by the side of the road while everyone else got home safely, an accusation frosted on John's features. Just like everything else, it would've been their fault.

She picked up the telephone, thought better of it, and put it back in its cradle. He'd call if he was stuck. And then, most likely, ask for Thomas. He wasn't interested, these days, in talking to her. She unloaded half of the plates from the dishwasher before realizing they were dirty. Then she loaded them back in, packed a scoop of soap into the door, and started the cycle. The gift cards they'd bought for John were under the tree, along with the requisite sweater and a pair of pajamas she knew he'd never wear. The house had to be prepared, but she'd already done most of the cleaning. Thomas had to deal with the sick alpaca, which he'd been putting off. Dinner would have to be orchestrated. Then, if there was time, she'd promised Sarah, the medical student who rented the garret apartment above their garage and who was *not* going home for the holiday (a catastrophic divorce, she'd told Joan, had made family more of an idea than anything else), that they'd move some wood over so she'd have enough to make it through the weekend. The garage was not attached, and stood fifty yards away from the house, obscured from view. Thomas would stack the wood when he got back. He would, Joan thought passingly, do anything for that girl. Sarah was, in her own awkward and plump and helpless way, appealing to men like him.

So the waiting began. Through the kitchen window, Joan could see the alpacas standing dumbly near the fence; the snow was starting to catch in their fur, and their large, expressive eyes were glued on the horizon, as if they were collectively willing some ancient, alpaca Godhead to materialize. Zachary—she'd named him after he'd become sick—was on his haunches, fifty feet away from the herd. She had tried nursing him back to health, warming bottles and feeding him like a newborn, but if that had helped, it had helped only marginally. The local country vet—who Joan secretly suspected despised her for the way they kept their animals (*recreational* was the word he'd used)—had been out and told her it was a lost cause. Joan refused to believe him at first—the guy'd barely left his truck before he was back in it, talking about all the other animals who required his attention that day—but soon after his visit Zachary had stopped eating, and when he moved, if he moved at all, it was with clear and unhappy effort. The herd, no fools, had begun to shun him, and at night his pathetic bleating entered her dreams. She'd wake, thinking she'd missed something important, had left someone stranded, or had otherwise failed in some meaningful way. Two evenings ago, unable to sleep, she'd left the house to sing, softly, to him; but then she'd seen Sarah peeking through her window and had become self-conscious. This was the animal kingdom, she reminded herself. Silly to see metaphor where there was none.

She heard Thomas coming downstairs and turned from the window to greet him. "That was John," he said when he came into the kitchen.

"I didn't hear the phone ring," she said.

"Cell phone."

"Oh," she said. Thomas walked halfway across the kitchen before remembering something upstairs. "Goddamn it, I'm unraveling," he said.

"You're just tired," she said. "I didn't sleep much either."

Thomas looked at her. His eyes were bagged. His beard, which she still wasn't used to, was neatly trimmed. "I'll be right back," he said. "It's his birthday on Thursday. I'd forgotten."

"I know his birthday," she said.

He would be thirty. For the last year he'd been calling in the middle of the night, waking them, sometimes with nothing to say, sometimes angry, sometimes crying. It happened once a month. Maybe more. It was impossible to say what he wanted, needed, from them. Thomas would take the phone across the hall, and talk to him until he calmed down. John never wanted to speak to her, not recently at least, and when she asked Thomas what they talked about he gave her an abbreviated, bare-bones account. The rest, he said, was nonsense, that John had just wanted someone's ear until he was tired enough to fall asleep. They'd been married for thirty-four years; she knew he was protecting her. She didn't like being shut out, it drove the two of them away from each other and into themselves; but after John's last visit, which had been frightening, and had shaken her, she was, at least partially, grateful for it. She was also grateful for Jocey, John's girlfriend. Since they'd been dating, the calls had become less frequent; where they'd failed to find a way to help him, it appeared she succeeded.

Thomas walked back into the kitchen, holding his hat. The scar on his forehead, just below his hairline, was healing well. The accident had happened two weeks ago, when Joan was running errands: Thomas, chopping wood, had yanked their axe out of the stump too quickly and brought the blunt end to his head, opening a deep cut. He'd knocked on Sarah's door, and she'd taken him inside and stitched him up. Joan had wanted to go to the hospital when she returned—when she saw his stitched forehead, his bloody bunched-up shirt on the floor—but Thomas insisted Sarah had closed it perfectly, and the hospital was unnecessary.

"So he's on his way?" Joan asked. "He knows about the storm?"

"Already on the road," Thomas said. "He does."

"Do you think they'll make it tonight?"

"I do."

"Good," Joan said. She wasn't sure if she meant it. "Do they have an emergency bag? Just in case?"

"He said they've got jackets, and jackets, and jackets. He wants to go skiing while they're here. I said that was fine." Thomas picked up an apple from the fruit bowl on the counter, inspected it, put it back down.

"Well, they've got a cell phone, at least."

"Yes. At least they've got that phone, thank God."

"You don't have to make fun of me," she said, and turned toward the window. The snow was coming heavier now.

Thomas moved to her side and rubbed small circles at the base of her neck. A comforting, nonsexual gesture. She wasn't used to the way he looked with a beard; it wasn't him, he'd never worn one; and for the last two weeks it had been a surprise, always, when he entered rooms. Another surprise: just this morning, she'd caught him masturbating in the shower. He'd apologized through the glass. When she'd asked him, later, and playfully she thought, what he'd been thinking about, he'd said, "Oh, nothing. You." She was embarrassed. She knew it wasn't true. What she imagined for him was an orgy of young women who looked just like Sarah, thirty upturned mouths, some bad music—but whatever image or scenario it was that he conjured, Thomas wouldn't say, and this morning, of all mornings, the inwardness of the action had upset her.

"I'm not making fun of you," he said. "You've barely slept. I wouldn't do that."

"All right," she said. "All right."

"I'm going to take Zachary down to the pit," he said. "You want to say good-bye?"

She shook her head. "No." Then she said, "I already did."

They stood near the window, looking out at the snow. "Call if you need anything," he said.

"I will," she said. Then she said, "Say hi to the nudist for me, if you see her."

She was talking about Sarah. It was a routine between them. Thomas squeezed Joan's hand, grabbed his keys from the peg by the door, and left the house. On a walk last summer, a few weeks after Sarah had moved in, he'd caught her swimming in the river near their property. He didn't realize—or, the word he'd used when telling Joan was *notice*—she was naked until he'd hailed her and begun a conversation. It wasn't true, of course. He had noticed, her nudity had stopped him dead in fact, but he didn't think about what he was doing—standing still, watching dumbly, and, the word had come later, peeping—until she'd looked up, started, and then, as she recognized him, relaxed, and put her hand over her naked heart. He'd been embarrassed; she, apparently, was not. She laughed, said something about not having a suit, and then waded to the bank and stood, nude, like some robust Greek emerging from a clamshell. One of her breasts was slightly larger than the other; on her hip was a scar like a holster. She'd asked Thomas to hand over her clothes, hanging on a branch behind him, which he'd done. Before he turned away, he caught sight of her stooping to step into her shorts and it had stilled him, even as he looked down the river to give her privacy. Midstream, there was a rock that was slowly parting the calm water, folding it over itself, and he concentrated on that until she'd said, okay.

He could've understood, and explained away, the sensation if it was merely desire. But it was larger than that. Seeing her exposed, and unafraid, had made him feel responsible for, and protective of, her. She knew very little about their troubles with John. Perhaps that was part of it. He knew Sarah felt affection for him, but also knew that was where it ended. He regretted telling Joan about seeing Sarah by the river. Recently, she'd confessed that she'd come to imagine Sarah as the daughter they'd never had: a successful, out-in-the-world-and-thriving child who offset the leaden feeling that congealed the air in the room whenever they talked about John. She didn't like that Sarah was waltzing around naked, for anyone to see. Right, Thomas had said. That's not what I was talking about, but right. That was five months ago, before John had become worse, before Sarah had stitched Thomas up. Before John's last visit. Before they'd decided, together, that relieving Zachary from the burden of his pain was the humane thing to do, and was, in fact, something required of them.

Outside, the clouds were low and gauzy, and walking across the lawn to the garage, Thomas put his hand on the hedge and realized that this day held only the promise of things he wasn't looking forward to: he didn't want to see his son, their only child, a man now, who had begun to view his entire life as someone else's fault; he didn't want to drive the dying alpaca to the pit, unceremoniously shoot it, and leave it to nature so they could present a home front untouched by sickness; and he didn't want to see Sarah. Earlier this morning, when Thomas had gone to the garage to take care of Zachary, there'd been a strange car, a red VW, in the driveway, parking him in. Someone visiting Sarah. This was a first. It was before dawn. Sarah's lights were still on, but he didn't knock. He didn't say: I'm blocked in down here. He'd stood near the car for a few minutes, feeling strangely deflated. Then he'd turned and walked, quietly, home. He would wait for whomever it was to leave. It was an intrusion he didn't like, but could do nothing about.

He was, however, looking forward to the storm. Deep snow, the kind they got in eastern Washington, dampened the landscape, rounding angles, muffling sound; everything became globular and remote, unrecognizable under the blanket. He wanted sloping drifts, up to the eaves. He wanted a crunch under his boots, the cold, granulated air in the back of his throat. Growing up, John had loved to shovel byzantine, snaking footpaths so one had to go first to the street, then in a small circle, and then, say, around the cherry tree in their front yard before getting to the car. Charming then. Indicative of character now.

The alpacas—there were ten of them—stood like a cluster of mops near the fence, away from Zachary, who was on the ground with his head nestled in a patch of grass, as if he were listening to the earth. "Hey, buddy," Thomas said as he approached. The alpaca stirred and let out a soft moan, then regained his stillness. The others would watch this taking away, Thomas knew, with the same slack-jawed and impenetrable apathy they greeted everything else.

"Ah, poor little guy," someone behind him said. He turned and saw Sarah. She was standing just outside the garage door, smoking a cigarette; he didn't know how he'd missed her. She wore only a thin, white undershirt, and sweatpants tucked into a pair of oversize Sorel boots, seemingly immune to the cold. She was in her late twenties, the same age as John, but looked, on account of her round face, younger. And healthier. Her long hair was pulled back into a messy ponytail.

"He'll be all right."

"No, he won't," she said, taking a deep drag and blowing it out. "Isn't that the point?"

A doctor who smokes. Thomas looked at the sick alpaca, and then back at Sarah. She wasn't wearing a bra, and he could see the dark outline of her nipples through her shirt. "Not exactly tee-shirt weather," he said before he could stop himself.

"Snow-mageddon!" she said cheerfully. She took another drag, and then nodded in the direction of the herd. "Some of those guys are pretty seriously dreadlocked. You should call them rasta-pacas."

"What-apacas?"

"Rasta. You know, like Bob Marley."

"Ah," Thomas said. "That works. I get it now."

Sarah stubbed her cigarette in the coffee can she kept outside for that purpose. Thomas walked over to the sick alpaca and roused him with a soft hand on his neck. The animal startled, then stood and allowed himself to be led to the trailer. Sarah watched with her arms folded over her chest. "It's brave of you to do this," she said when Thomas had the animal near the gate. Upon seeing the trailer Thomas had hitched to the back of his truck, Zachary teetered, then dropped to his haunches. Sarah kneeled, and took Zachary's blank face in her hands as if, Thomas thought, to kiss it.

"I don't know if *brave* is the right word," he said back.

Sarah stood, reached into the pocket of her sweatpants, emerged with another cigarette, and lit it. "That vet's an asshole. You shouldn't have to do this alone."

"He couldn't be bothered with it until after Christmas, apparently," Thomas said. "Joan and I talked about it. It doesn't seem right to wait that long. This is something we can do. Something I can do. He's in pain. We discussed it."

"You want me to come?"

Thomas looked at the alpaca. "It's going to be messy, I think," he said.

Sarah snorted. "You don't know messy. Try the ER. Try arterial blood. Try a bunch of maniac drunks trying to kill each other in the waiting room. Blood doesn't bother me." She smiled, and looked at him. "As you know."

"We," Thomas said, "your legion of lucky patients."

"Lucky indeed. That's me. Dr. Luck. That's what I'll be called."

"It's going to be cold," Thomas said. "And probably awful. I can handle it."

"Let's not worry about it," Sarah said. She stubbed her second cigarette on top of the first. "I don't have much else to do. I'll get my coat."

As she disappeared back into the garage, Thomas hushed the sick animal into the trailer and closed the gate behind him. Zachary nestled down in the center of the trailer as he had in the field, as if, Thomas thought, he knew the sort of remoteness required of him now. Thomas could hear Sarah clomping up the garage steps, heard her door closing. He looked up to her window—he'd wave her off, say thanks but forget it—but the shade was drawn. Maybe her company would be welcome after all. It would prevent him, at least, from thinking too much about John. He dropped his keys in the cab of his truck, went back inside the house. He yelled good-bye up the stairs to Joan, and retrieved one of his shotguns out of the gun cabinet on the first floor. When he came back, Sarah was already sitting in the passenger seat, and the two of them drove, with the sick alpaca, out of the driveway, and away from the house.

Suicide, Ma, John had said on the phone to Joan three months ago. *Don't you ever think about it?* Once she heard this, the receiver she'd been holding to her head had suddenly turned heavy and cold on her ear. John had been talking about his new obsession: the death of a childhood hero, a musician who'd stabbed himself in the heart, collapsed in a bathtub, and hadn't been found for seven days. *That guy, he had the whole world in his hands. And decided to end it. So tell me what I've got? Why are you so sure I'm going to pan out?* He went on, digressing here and there, grandstanding, and backtracking. It was manipulative talk, but John had always had a bit of that in him. This conversation was different, both aimless and purposeful, and she didn't recognize where it was coming from. It felt stagey, mobilized to elicit a response which, she knew from past experience, would only send him further down his own private rabbit hole. Nothing she said was ever "right"; nothing she'd ever said to John had been "right." Her therapist had told her she ought to take the things her son said both seriously (engage with the ideas presented) and not seriously (not to let those ideas infect their relationship). What relationship? she'd wanted to say. I'm a life-support machine here, all tubes and knobs. Fuzzed-out beeps, posing as sentences with a life of their own.

They hadn't done much to John's room since he'd left for college, and Joan now stood leaning against the doorframe, looking in, as if there were an invisible line in the carpet that separated where he'd slept from the rest of the house. The posters he'd put on the walls with rubber cement still hung slightly off center; the news articles he'd carefully clipped and pinned to his bulletin board, though yellowed now with age and brittle, were undisturbed. He'd wanted it kept that way. This was the room where they talked to him during the night. Or, rather, where Thomas talked to him. After long nights, bad nights, she'd find Thomas diagonal on John's bed, phone resting on his chest, an expression that looked like anger, or, sometimes, sadness, caulked onto his sleeping face.

It was almost one o'clock. Joan crossed the threshold and finished her tour of what she and Thomas had begun calling the amber museum, straightening pillows, making the bed—it was a single, almost child-size, she had no idea how both John and his new girlfriend were going to share it, but that was their intention—and then she surveyed the room. John's posters and clippings—of overdosed and dead musicians and obscure Japanese movies; reports of unsolved crimes and natural disasters, sunken ships raised to the surface—these things told her nothing she wanted, needed, to know. Surely, these chosen artifacts were important, these records of her son; surely they were clues a careful and loving parent could assemble to glimpse the whole. But she couldn't piece them together. She had no clarity, overwhelmed, as she was, by the desire for him to be all right. All right. Whatever that meant.

He was smart. He always had been. He'd gone to a good and expensive college, where he'd won awards for his art projects. But he'd never been happy. He'd never stayed in one place very long, but until recently they'd understood his restlessness to be a symptom of what he called his high standard of living: he simply wasn't content following the crowd, doing what everyone else was doing. But now, some sort of switch had flipped. He called when he got a job; he called when he quit, or lost it. He complained about the pressure everyone put on him. He called when his friends paired off, and stopped talking to him. He called when he was out of money. They gave it to him, and endured his resentment. Thomas had reassured her that this was just a phase; that he would grow out of it, that he would straighten his course on his own. But here he was, thirty years old. And here they were, trying to convince themselves nothing was wrong.

She went to the window. The snow had begun to stick. The room was in good shape. It was whisper quiet. It was, she thought with some satisfaction and some sadness, just the way he liked it. John's favorite song, when he'd been small, had been "What Do We Do with a Drunken Sailor?" Now the melody came back to her, and, standing at the window, she hummed some fragments. She'd never liked the violence of the song, but what stuck with her this time was the question that began the refrain—what do we do? What do we do. The alpacas, who had not moved, and who would not move unless prodded, were turning white with the weather. They did not appear to mourn the missing.

What had happened in September, the last time John was home, was this: they'd invited Sarah for dinner. They hadn't thought much about it at the time—how John would react, showing up late as usual, the drive always taking him longer than anyone expected, upon seeing the three of them sitting around the table, already halfway through the meal. But they had waited to eat until it was too rude to Sarah not to. Thomas brought the phone to the table, said eat, eat, why not. As it was, the food was cold by the time they sat down. They'd finish the meal, and then, after Sarah had gone, reheat it for John when he arrived.

But he'd shown up middinner. Walked in the door with his bags, looked at the scene in front of him—everyone around the table, Sarah in his seat—and said, *So this is the famous doctor? I've heard some things about you*. She'd asked him what kind of things, and he'd shrugged, and said, *You know what doctors do? They make healthy people feel better about themselves*.

You're late, John, Joan had said. We just sat down. It's no one's fault. Don't be rude.

Roads were bad, he'd said, still looking at Sarah. *I'm just talking. I'm not being rude.*

Sarah had tried her best to recover—everyone had, Thomas getting up from the table to get a plate, Joan saying how good it was to see him, Sarah explaining she wasn't a doctor yet, but could pass on some terrible doctor stories if he was interested. John had remained in the doorway, slack-faced and thinner than Joan remembered until Thomas came to take his bags. Apparently satisfied by the effect of his arrival, John shoved his hands deep in his pockets and went quiet, radiating a strange, barely coiled aggression that was unrecognizable to both Joan and Thomas. He walked over to where Sarah and Joan were still seated, politely pulled out a chair at the table, and began complimenting the food he hadn't yet eaten. Thomas wasn't sure if he smelled alcohol on his son or not. By the time the meal was over, a pall had descended over the four of them, and the discussion, when there was any, was stilted and vague. They knew why they'd invited Sarah, and they realized their mistake, suddenly plain to everyone. They'd invited her because they hadn't wanted to be alone with their son.

The following morning, Sarah called early, upset, to say that the door to the henhouse near the garage was unlatched and open. She thought the worst, but had been afraid to look herself. There were coyotes in the area, they'd lost chickens before; but this time the coop had been locked. Thomas was sure of that. He left the house knowing what he was going to find, hoping he was wrong. The door to the coop stood wide open. Half the chickens were missing. Feathers covered the ground like snow. It hadn't been coyotes. In the center of the coop lay a single dead chicken, its neck twisted and broken. There wasn't much blood. John's car was gone. He'd left before anyone was awake.

Thomas found a hen outside the coop, near the garage,

and picked her up. She made no move to get away, offered no resistance in his arms, but she was not calmed by his whispering. He saw Joan watching him through the kitchen window. He thought about calling the police, and knew as he thought it that he would not. He would tell Sarah it had been coyotes; that he had forgotten to latch the gate. He would tell Joan the truth, but he wouldn't let her see it. Later that night, John called, sobbing, and Thomas said, *It's okay, it's okay.* John said he hadn't meant to frighten anyone, and Thomas comforted him, said okay.

The pit was twenty miles to the southeast. The roads were empty, and as they drove Sarah twisted the radio dial, looking for a station that wasn't wrapped up in storm tracking. She settled on a country station, and turned it down. As they'd pulled out of the driveway, Sarah had asked him how the law practice was going, but that conversation wrapped itself up quickly. Now they were on a road that continued to Montana, driving in what Thomas called the Farm Truck—a rusted old Tacoma he'd bought years ago, had repainted, and drove whenever they were transporting animals, doing dump runs, or otherwise trying to fit in around town. Sometimes, when John called, Thomas would leave the house just to sit in this truck while he listened to his son. The clutch, when engaged, hummed and clunked. The cab smelled like old boots. He liked that smell. He liked the way it blended, now, with whatever perfume Sarah was wearing.

Finally she switched the radio off and turned in her seat. "So John's coming in today, right? Joan told me a while ago you were expecting him."

"He is," Thomas said. There was a muffled thud from the trailer, and he slowed down. "With his girlfriend."

"Ah-ha," she said. "So I don't need to come for dinner, then."

"Right," Thomas said. "We didn't figure you'd want to."

"No. I've got plans," Sarah said. "You know, most people love doctors. He didn't like me very much."

"It's not you. He's got other things going on. It's not you."

"What kind of other things?"

Thomas sighed. He adjusted the heater on the dashboard. "We don't really know, I guess."

"Is he seeing anyone now? You know, a therapist?"

"No," Thomas said. "Well, yes. Sort of. The last one figured out some sort of medication regimen that seems to be working for him. I think the girlfriend has helped."

"Joan told me you guys talk a lot."

"More like, he talks."

"Are you worried about him?"

Thomas gripped the steering wheel. This wasn't what he wanted to talk about. He wanted to know who had been visiting her, blocking him in, but he didn't know how to bring it up. "Worried like how?"

"I don't know," Sarah said. She was absently chewing one of her fingers. "Do you think it's helped? I don't— I'm not trying to pry. Not my business."

"The therapist helped," Thomas said. "Jocey's helped.

The medicine's helped." He felt his throat tightening. "It's hard to know what he wants sometimes. It'll straighten out. He will, that is. I'd rather not talk about it. That's all I've been doing. Talking."

Sarah adjusted in her seat. "Got it," she finally said. "I'm glad things are working out."

They went back to driving in silence. The heater was cranked and pushing hot air directly into Thomas's face. He took his hat off, tossed it on the dash, and adjusted the vent. Sarah, Joan. John, for Christmas. He cleared his throat. "So you've got plans tonight?"

"I do." She'd been digging around in her pockets, and stopped. "Now, that," she said, "that's healing nicely."

At first Thomas was confused. Then he remembered—his forehead, the stitching, the scar. "It is," he said. He lowered his head so she could get a better look. As she leaned over the center console, he brought his speed down. He'd taken the stitches out four days ago, in the mirror with sterilized tweezers like Sarah had instructed.

"Very nice," she said.

"Something to be proud of," Thomas said. He was glad the conversation had picked up again, had moved past John. He glanced at the road, then brought his eyes back to hers. Her lips were pursed. "You can barely see it," he said.

Sarah unfastened her seat belt, and moved closer to study the scar. When he'd shown up, bloody, at her door, she'd been so concerned. She had guided him inside her apartment, sat him down in the kitchen. Wiped the blood away gently with a wet and warm towel, applied pressure. Took his face in her hands to inspect the wound and then decided, if he was up for it, that she could stitch him up right then and there. She'd given him painkillers and a small shot of anesthetic so he wouldn't feel the needle. And he hadn't felt it, not exactly. He'd closed his eyes. He could feel pressure and tugging and knew the wound was coming together.

"You should see the wood," he'd said, a joke.

"I believe it," she'd said back.

At night, while talking—or, rather, listening—to John, he would return to this surgery again and again, rolling the memory around in his head like a marble. The rhythmic tugging. Their proximity. She had been able to help him, in a concrete way. It had been so simple. At one point he'd reached out, put his hand on her hip to brace himself, and she'd let it rest there. Her skin was warm. He could feel her hip bone in conversation with the rest of her body as she concentrated on her work. When, periodically, she'd reached behind him for the faucet, her loose shirt brushed against his upturned face. Thomas had sat with his eyes closed, his hand more alive than any other part of his body. He had loved the touch of her skin. Sarah was professional and quick, and had patted him on the shoulder when she was finished, the way dentists, postcavity, do. The whole thing was over before it had begun.

Now, in the truck, they were close again. *If you would reach out,* he thought. *If you would just reach out, I can handle whatever's coming next.* And then she did just that, a quick, darting gesture, her hand on the side of his face, her thumb compressing, lightly, the skin near the wound. Thomas felt her breath on the side of his face. "Not bad," she said.

He was now going well below the speed limit. He hadn't seen any other traffic, did not see why this wouldn't be allowed, but behind him, suddenly, there was honking. He sat up straighter and looked in his side mirror. A red pickup was almost on the gate of his trailer. Thomas slowed even more, rolled down his window, and motioned for the truck to pass. As the driver pulled parallel, Thomas looked over, just in time to see the man in the passenger seat move his eyes from him to Sarah. He was dressed in red and white camouflage. He looked vaguely familiar.

"Do you know that guy?" Thomas said. The truck had slowed to Thomas's speed. Sarah said nothing. The man rapped at his own window, then made a gun with his fingers and pointed it at the two of them. Then the rust-gutted truck was speeding ahead into the distance, weaving in and out of lanes, as if driving a cone course. "Weird," Sarah said. They'd been silent while it happened.

"Someone oughta shoot his tires out," Thomas said after a few minutes.

"Someone will," Sarah said. "Eventually."

The flowers Joan had bought and placed on the mantel were already beginning to wilt. She turned the vase, stood back, turned it again. Yesterday, she had talked to her therapist about John, hoping he could help her out of what, in the last few days, had become a panic. Children aren't going to be what you want them to be, he said. I don't want him to be anything! she said back. Tears again. Some people, he said, just need more time. When she asked him how much time was enough, he fixed her over his desk, and said that was something she ought to think about. "When he talks—what he says—it's like an infection, like an earache. I can't get it out of my head," she said. "It has the ring of verdict to it."

"But you've told me"—here he flipped his notes, to make sure. "The two of you have stopped talking. That he only talks to your husband, now."

"When we talked," she corrected. The last time she'd been on the phone with John, the last time he'd asked for her, she had been unable to give him what he needed, and he had said: *I'm thinking maybe you don't love me.* And at the moment he said it, at the very moment the words were out of his mouth and coiling toward her over the line, it had been true. He had *made* it true. Now, lying in bed, she would listen to Thomas down the hall, saying yes, or no, mumbling inaudibly so it sounded as if the floor itself was humming softly with the murmur of her husband's voice. Sometimes, unable to sleep, she would imagine John's side of the conversation, and in her head this would become a conversation between her and her husband, the conversation they never had, a constantly invoked What have we done? To what degree is this our fault? How much longer will this take?

"You're confessing this to me. He sounds like he's confessing to you," her therapist had said. He cleared his throat.

"I don't think it's love he's after," she said.

"Then, what?"

"It feels," she said, "more like he's looking for confirmation. Like he's . . . begging us. For something. Some confirmation that his problems are bigger than we are. And that he wants us to prove it to him. To confirm it. I don't know."

Her therapist had put his pen down, folded his arms, and made a bad-smell face. "That," he said, "doesn't sound quite right to me. We've only been seeing each other for a few months, and it's possible I'm not getting a handle on John. But that doesn't sound quite right."

This kind man, Joan thought. Letting her talk like this. Of course he wasn't getting a handle on her son. *They* didn't have a handle on him. But she hadn't helped; she hadn't told this man everything; she hadn't fully confessed, if that was the right word. She hadn't told him about the chicken Thomas found. She hadn't told him how at thirteen, John's eyes, which had always, she thought, appeared dilated, went hard, and seemed to demand a distance from her that she'd perhaps too easily granted. How, at fourteen, he'd cuffed her left ear and Thomas had had to wrestle him to the ground, and from the kitchen floor, under his father, John had cried until he choked. She'd made Thomas promise never to hurt John again; and then she'd asked him to apologize. He'd done both. And now, when talking to this man, her therapist, she simply described John, growing up, as too observant for his own good, too hard on himself. A boy whose loneliness transformed one day into sarcasm and then into a strange, emotional cruelty. She regretted having only one child, she said. She thought a brother, or a sister, might've helped. Maybe they shouldn't have moved so far away from other people, into the country, like they had done. She was protecting her son from this man, and what he might say. It wasn't the point of these sessions, she knew that. But just as she was secretly relieved that Thomas hadn't called the police on John, had acted, in fact, as if he had never set foot in that chicken coop, she took a shameful pride in not giving this man the full story. Mothers protect their sons.

John, at four, giving her a red Play-Doh heart he'd sculpted at school for her birthday, which she'd hardened in the oven and, with a piece of ribbon, made into a necklace and worn on that day every year since. At seven, learning to ride one of their old horses, coming back inside on a fall day, sweaty and elated, asking her if she'd seen him do it. You don't let go of those things, she thought. You can't. They don't release you.

"Joan," her therapist had said. He wasn't accusing her of not loving her son. He wouldn't go that far.

"That's because it isn't," she said.

Thomas's phone rang as they were pulling into a gas station. The road had widened into a four-lane, and as they'd begun passing little convenience stores, roadhouse bars, and a Mc-Donald's, Thomas had put the wipers against the snow. Sarah kept her hands in her lap. She didn't mention the scar again. The storm was picking up but didn't appear to have the steam that had been promised. The first stoplight they'd come to was near the paper mill, and as they waited for the light to turn, a smell like old eggs came in through the heater. He parked near the pump and cut the engine before answering. "Dad?" his son said. "It's John." This was how all their conversations started. As if there could be anyone else who called him that.

"John," he said. "How's the driving?"

"I'm about two hours away, I think," John said. "The snow's coming down, though. Making it slow. Snow-mageddon casualties. Car crashes. Ascension. Blood on the road, and all that."

"All right." Blood on the road? Thomas looked at Sarah. She'd unbuckled her seat belt and was reaching behind her for her coat. Out back, he could hear the alpaca, evidently roused, kicking the side of the trailer.

John cleared his throat. "You in the car?"

Thomas nodded, then remembered he was on the phone. "Groceries," he said. "Last minute." He wasn't going to tell John about Zachary. In the background, Thomas could hear someone else. Or maybe it was the radio. The connection wasn't good. It seemed, to Thomas, that the two of them were talking through strung-together cans.

"Well, how's this for a turn of events: Jocey's not coming. I've got her car, I'm driving in it, but she's not coming."

"That's not her in the car with you?"

"No."

"Everything all right?" Thomas said. "I was looking forward to meeting her." The alpaca was really kicking now; tin heavy thumps reverberated through the cab of the truck.

There was silence on John's end. "Bet you were," he said

finally. "My car's not working right now. You better tell Mom. All that dinner planning and stuff. The agonizing over who sits where. Because she's Mom."

"She's just going to be happy to see you," Thomas said.

John snorted. "I don't know about that," he said. "She'll probably be happy about Jocey, and the decisions Jocey felt necessitated to make."

"I don't think so, John," Thomas said. "What happened?"

More silence. Then John said, "Ruination."

Jesus Christ, John, Thomas thought. John's car, the one they'd given him, was two years old. "Does she know you have her car?"

"I knew you'd ask that," John said, and snorted. "Yes, in fact, she does. She gave it to me. A parting gift." Thomas decided not to answer. John continued: "So the three of us. Maybe you should invite God's Gift to Medicine for dinner. We'll see how that plays the second time around." Sarah opened her door, stepped out, and slammed it shut. Thomas felt his face flush. He watched her make her way into the gas station's food-mart, and wave at the kid at the register.

"Who's with you, Dad? Is that her? That her in the car with you? I heard a door slam. Did she hear what I said? Put her on the phone."

"John, what's the problem?"

"No problem," he said. "Why?"

"We're looking forward to seeing you. Jocey or no Jocey."

"Well, good," he said. Then he said, "Here's a problem. Answer me this problem, if you want. I do everything I can for everybody, and it always fucks up. I do everything I can to get people's attention, to hold it, and I get nothing." It sounded to Thomas like John might be crying.

"You have our attention, John."

"No," he said. He *is* crying, Thomas thought. But his voice was rising, not getting weaker. "No. All you do is listen and nod. I could do anything. And you listen and nod."

"That's not true, John," Thomas said. "I'm trying to help. If I listen, I'm helping. What do you want me to do?"

John's voice faded, as if he had taken the phone away from his face. Thomas couldn't quite hear him. It sounded like he was giving instructions to someone else in the car, but no second voice answered. Then, suddenly, he was back. "You know what I want for Christmas this year? Old times."

"Old times?"

"You heard me." John was talking softly now. "I want, fucking, old times."

Maybe John was drinking. On the road, and drinking. Thomas saw that Sarah was coming back from the food-mart, holding two cups of coffee. He got out of the truck, pointed to the phone, signaled that she should get back in.

"You still there, Pops?" John said. "Still there?"

"I heard you," Thomas said. He was walking, now, away from the truck, and away from Zachary. The traffic on the road, suddenly busy, made a wet noise that kept him from hearing John clearly. "Old times."

"That," John said, "and I want to see that doctor you've got above the garage."

Thomas stopped. He was fifty feet from the road. He looked, saw his truck, and the trailer, but couldn't see Sarah in the cab.

John's voice was picking up strength. "Right? Maybe spend the night over there. See if she can tell me why this, shit keeps happening to me."

Thomas drew a deep breath, and felt the cold on the back of his throat. He shifted the phone from one hand to the other. "I don't think so, John," he said, and shoved his cold hand into his jacket pocket. "I don't think so."

"And why not?" John said. The radio in his car was suddenly silent. "Isn't she perfect for me? Isn't that what you want?"

"No," Thomas said. "No, John, she's not."

"Well," he said, "I'm single and available, and I'll be there soon. I want answers. This is fresh stuff I'm talking about here. Heartache. I think we all want answers."

"You've got—" Thomas began, but stopped. His jacket felt tight. He had nothing to say.

"Well, look at that," John said. "That doesn't sound like a nod from here."

Thomas felt a pressure in his ears, a dull pain that began at his jaw and clustered at his temple. He pulled the phone away from his head. John was still talking. For what felt like years Thomas had endured nights of badgering like this, had waded into an endless abyss of silent listening. He'd cajoled and placated John; dodged his accusations, done what he could to mitigate the self-pity and anger as John went up and down, even though it was never clear to Thomas where he'd slipped up as a parent and a friend, where he'd fallen short. He'd come to terms with feeling responsible for things not working out the way they were supposed to. For John not working out the way he was supposed to. He absorbed everything John said like a distant dark star so it wouldn't radiate any farther than it already did. Beyond that, he didn't know what to do. But there must be a limit to all of this. He swallowed a shoot of saliva, and brought the phone back to his ear.

"Give me one reason she isn't," John said. "I can wait." There was no mistaking his tone, this time. It was a threat. The texture of John's voice on the phone sounded different to Thomas—it had become thicker, angrier. Thomas could feel desperation rising in his body. They had been approaching this moment for a long time now, and it had finally arrived. It was clear: this kid—their son—he would take everything if they let him. And he would keep taking. The desperation was turning to panic. Perhaps he and Joan were to blame for all of this, perhaps that was true. Perhaps they could have tried harder to help their son. Perhaps they had tried too hard. But that would have to wait. For now, the connection with John needed to be cut. Thomas looked up the road, back from where they'd come. At the end of it was their home. At the end of it there was a language John would understand. "Because, John," he said, and took a breath. "Because she's mine."

There was a deep silence on John's end. To Thomas it sounded like both a gathering and a negation of thought; the moment after the instruments tune and resolve in communal quiet. "John," Thomas said. "Listen to me. Don't bring your problems home this time."

"I knew it," John said. He was whispering now. "I knew it. You want her so bad. You old, bearded goat, and I got you to say it." A pause. Then, suddenly cheerful, he said, "Secret's safe, Pops. She's all yours. You know me." Then the line went dead.

Thomas held the phone to his ear for a full minute before gently closing and placing it back in his pocket. He walked back to his truck, set the gas nozzle in the tank, and hooked the handle. What he wanted, now, was quiet forever. He felt gone from himself, deep in some ocean. Years of tending, and without warning, he'd slipped. What he'd said could not be taken back. What John thought he knew would not be forgotten. It didn't matter if it was true or not.

Zachary was quiet, staring at the traffic through the slats in the trailer. The snow clouds stretched in pregnant monochrome across the sky. Sarah was waiting with the coffee in the cab of the truck. Thomas got in. When Sarah had stitched the gash in his forehead, she'd told him to hold still, and swung one of her legs between his, as if to hold him, sitting, in place. She had fixed him to his chair. He'd wanted to take one of her breasts, not inches from his upturned chin, in his mouth. He'd never wanted to leave.

He turned the key halfway in the ignition, and the radio came to life. *Blood on the road*. He took his hands from the wheel, leaned back deep into the headrest, and closed his eyes.

"What's wrong?" Sarah said. "Hey, what is it? Is John okay?"

Thomas opened his eyes. The windshield was dirty with road-salt and snow. Everything outside of the truck looked cold. Sarah was looking at him, holding their coffee cups. "What is it?" she said again, more softly this time.

"Please," he said. He had meant to ask her a question, but found he couldn't.

"Please what?" she said.

"Nothing," he said, "nothing at all." They sat for a minute without saying anything more. And then he reached for her. He felt as if he were moving slowly, but knew that wasn't the case. His jacket caught briefly on the armrest, and the center console pushed uncomfortably against his ribs. He felt his hand and fingers behind her neck, under her hair, as he pulled her toward him. He'd meant to bring them face-to-face, to kiss her he thought, that was, he knew, what he wanted, but then he saw her expression—disbelief, terror; a child, she looked like a child—and he brought her head to his chest instead.

He had no idea how long they stayed like that. He was aware only that after a time she was gently pulling away from him, and he was keeping her there. "Thomas," she said into his jacket, and he reached to put his other arm around her. "Thomas," she said again, harshly this time. Then, suddenly, she wrenched free.

He felt a pain spread out along his thigh, one that bloomed just above his kneecap, and radiated up his leg. He looked down. The coffee from the cup she'd been holding had spilled in his lap, a dark, pulsing stain. He looked back to Sarah; she had pressed herself against the passenger door, as far away from him as she could get. The left side of her face was reddened, had chafed against his jacket; the right side drained of blood. A few strands of her hair were in her mouth.

"I'm sorry," she said. She was looking at his lap. "Sorry."

His leg was throbbing. His vision had cleared. "Don't be," he said back.

The wood was stacked behind their house, near the now empty chicken coop, and with nothing else to do inside—wanting, in fact, to get out of the house—Joan had put on her coat and boots, grabbed the canvas log holder they kept by the kitchen door, and braced herself against the weather. Their entire property appeared still under the new blanket. The flakes falling from the sky were large; she could hear the sound of them as they hit and stuck. She walked halfway to the woodpile and stopped to enjoy it.

Her plan was to move the wood out of the weather and fill the log basin by their fireplace, so it would be dry enough to catch and no one would have to trudge out later for more. After that, she'd set some aside in the garage for Sarah.

The first bundle she overloaded, and couldn't pick up. As she pulled some of the bigger pieces from the pile, she felt a presence, and started. When she turned, she saw the herd of alpacas, standing near the fence, watching her. They were covered in snow; they looked both mournful and resilient. She'd bought them on a whim two years ago, with some idea toward selling their fur. She regretted it now. She regretted everything now. When they'd bought this place thirty years ago, she'd been sure they'd eventually outgrow it; it was a small house. But now, with the light coming out of the kitchen window, burning soft and warmly through the falling snow, it felt, if anything, too large. They were turning into hermits, she and Thomas; their house a monument to failure and quiet and shame. They barely talked. It was a house full of empty rooms and hallways, cheerful family pictures taken by strangers.

It was three o'clock. Both John and Thomas were now overdue. Inside, the table was set. The ham she'd picked out, the ham she deliberated over in the grocery store for far longer than necessary, as if there were some secret to be found in the weight of the thing, was defrosting. Jocey—whoever this girl was—would be a hedge against John's heavy pull. They would simply ask her questions, and then the night would be over.

On her way back into the kitchen with the wood, she miscalculated the width of the entryway, and with all the weight of the load caught her fingers on the doorframe. Her vision went white; the firewood fell like clattering bowling pins to the kitchen floor. "Goddamn it," she said. She put her hands between her legs and squeezed. A few of the logs had rolled outside and were now propping the kitchen door open. She kicked those out of the way, closed the door, and, still in her jacket, went to the sink.

The water took some of the pain away. She turned the faucet off, and braced herself on the counter. No one prepares you for this, she thought. There's always some way to mess up. And it was then that she looked out the window and saw an unfamiliar car, a blue sedan, in their driveway. It sat at the far end, almost fifty yards away, where the driveway connected with the street. It was idling; Joan could see exhaust puffing into the cold like tiny distress signals. Someone, maybe, waiting for Sarah. Though why make her walk through the weather? Using her left hand she gathered the wood from the floor and put it back in the carrier, and then brought it into the living room. The rest of the wood-getting would have to wait. She tried calling Thomas, but he didn't pick up. When she went back to the window, the car was gone.

In the living room now, she built a fire and lit it. Her fingers ached only dully. As the kindling took, she flipped on the television, hoping for news of the weather. They were broadcasting clips of people in the snow: kids rolling down a hill; a huge truck with a makeshift plow hitched to its front; abandoned vehicles wedged into snowbanks like icebound ships. These were scenes from the highway, but a few hours east, where the storm had settled down in earnest. The newscast cut to a man in a snowsuit pointing out cars that were sliding sideways through intersections in a small town that looked like every other small town. The vehicles turned and slid so slowly that Joan wanted to say, What's the problem here? Just get out of the truck and stop it with your hands. She clicked it off.

When she went to the window again, she was surprised to see the blue car had returned.

* * *

The pit was nothing but a large meadow off the highway. It was hidden by a ridge of evergreens, accessible only by a small paved road that after a few sharp inclines turned to dirt. It was no one's property. Thomas had been here once before, and had been told by a neighbor who kept cows that it was an unofficial dumping ground, a small, farm-animal graveyard. The road was unplowed but still drivable. As Thomas pulled to a stop, there was a sound from the rig as if Zachary were pitching himself from one side of the trailer to the other.

He was alone. Sarah had stayed at the gas station. Before Thomas had pulled away, she'd walked inside the food-mart and returned with napkins. She handed them to Thomas through the window of the truck. "That could be really bad," she'd said.

"I'm fine," he'd replied. He took the napkins, and laid them carefully on his leg. The cold air from the window helped. Then he apologized. She nodded, as if she wasn't quite listening.

"Let me at least give you a ride home," he'd said. He wanted to explain himself if he could. A huge mistake. All of it. "How are you going to get back?" The snow was coming thickly and had already covered the wipers.

"I'm going to call someone," she'd said.

She disappeared again through the doors of the food-mart, and Thomas drove away. A mile down the road, he pulled into the parking lot of a Rite-Aid and sat there for what could've been fifteen minutes or an hour. He had no idea.

Now, at the pit, Thomas opened his door and eased himself out of the truck. The meadow in front of him looked like a wide lake, frozen over. He limped around to the back of the trailer. He didn't want to do this now. Zachary stood with his back to Thomas, near the wheel-well, leaning against the wall. Thomas bent down, scooped up a handful of snow, pressed it against his leg, and held it there. With his other hand, he reached into his jacket pocket for his phone.

"I've been calling you," Joan said. "What happened?"

"I know," Thomas said. "I'm sorry. I'm here. With Zachary."

"Is Sarah with you?"

The snow in Thomas's hand began to melt down his leg. "No," he said. "No, she's not."

"There's a car here, waiting for her. In the driveway."

Thomas switched the phone to his other hand. "Joan," he said. "Joan, I don't know what to tell you."

"It's not John. Whoever it is keeps coming and going," Joan said. "It's here now. The car. Just sitting at the end of the driveway. It's been coming and going for the last hour."

"What color is it? Red?"

"Blue."

Thomas could hear his wife moving around their house. He imagined her at the living room window, peering out. The sun was beginning to go down.

"I tried calling Sarah," Joan said. "She didn't pick up."

"She's at a gas station," Thomas said. "Down the road."

"Why? I don't—"

"Joan," Thomas said. "It's probably John. I talked to him a little while ago. He's driving someone else's car."

He heard the oven timer go off. She must be in the kitchen. "If it's John, why isn't he coming in?"

"I don't know, Joan. I don't know."

Zachary, in the trailer, began scratching at the floor. Then he hutched up and put his head down. "Joan," Thomas said. "I talked to him. I think he's worse."

"Worse," she said. "What do you mean?"

"Joan, I made a mistake. I think you should lock the doors."

"I'm not going to lock the doors on my own—"

"Joan," Thomas said. "Trust me. Lock him out. He's old enough. It's what you want, I know that. It's what I want. Don't let him in the house."

"It's not—you're not making sense, Thomas. You have to tell me what's going on."

"Joan," he said. "You know it's him. It couldn't be anyone else. Jocey isn't with him."

There was silence on the line. All this talking, Thomas thought, punctuated by silences large enough to drown in. "I'm on my way home," he said. "I'll be home soon." He pulled the phone away from his ear and cut the call.

The day was almost over. Thomas unlatched the trailer, reached for Zachary's lead, and drew him up. He walked with him until they were in the middle of the meadow, then let go of the lead. He put his hand on the animal's back. Zachary watched the trees, fifty yards away. They stood like that for a while, then Thomas turned and limped back to his truck for the shotgun. He told himself that if Zachary had wandered away by the time he got to the door of his truck, if he'd made any attempt to move at all, he wasn't going to shoot him. *That,* he thought, *is the kind of person I want to be.*

He opened the passenger door, leaned in, pulled the gun off its rack, and turned. Zachary hadn't budged. Thomas shut the door, and walked toward the feeble, ancient-looking animal, breaking the gun as loudly as he could. A bird of some kind took flight behind him. Thomas took two shells from his breast pocket and thumbed them home. He moved until he was ten feet from Zachary, and stopped. He felt like he wanted to scream. His pant leg was frozen and stiff, and there was an absence of feeling in his leg. The snow fell like static. They would, all three of them, talk this out. They would get past this. Thomas looked once directly into Zachary's eyes, nestled the butt of the shotgun on his shoulder, and raised the barrel. The alpaca stood there, waiting to be shot.

camp winnesaka

The thing is, we were worried about enrollment. We were already way down for the summer, thanks to video games and league sports. Who knows what else. Over-concerned parents, maybe, worried about their kid falling behind the little engineers in India and China, etc., which I'm not discounting, you do have to think of the future. But that's the climate we were facing, so in terms of what some of you are calling the Debacle . . .

There are things I'm sorry about. Things that probably could've been handled better. But everyone makes mistakes. That's the first thing we tell our campers when they arrive in the Condor Transports: mistakes happen, but you have to keep the big picture in mind. You have to remain optimistic in your decision making. You have to value intent. And if intentions are on the up and up?

It started with Moosey, the moose head that's hung over the mantel in the Chow Hut for Lord knows how long, and who has, over the years, become our unofficial mascot. Spirits were low with this batch of campers, I don't know why. We just had a higher number of pasty, sort of obese kids sign up this summer for some reason. They got a kick out of Moosey, but it was hard to get them excited about much else. Any other year, maybe it wouldn't have been such a big deal, but this year, with the enrollment issue, it was different. There are four other camps around Lake Oboe, and parents visit during the summer. If they like what they see, chances are they'll sign their kids up for another session, which takes a load off our back in terms of marketing. But everywhere the parents—we call them Pen Pals—looked this year, it was sullen city. The kids weren't taking care of their Teepees. The Spirit Catchers they made in arts and crafts looked like they'd been weaved by retards. We staged a Capture the Coonskin game, and it was like watching apathy battle indecision. A PR disaster, essentially.

So the visiting Pen Pals see this, and go, Why should we send our kids here next year instead of one of the *other* camps? And to that I found myself saying, Good question. I really found myself saying that. It was depressing.

And then, one day, Moosey was gone. And the campers . . . well, they were upset. We were all upset. No one knew who'd taken the thing. I didn't think it could've been one of our kids, but we did a bunk search anyway. We combed the beach. Had the campers stomp through the brambles, arms linked so they wouldn't miss a spot. They didn't find him.

The fact that someone could just *take* Moosey, it was a little more than some of the campers could bear. To be honest, it was a little more than I could bear. Things *already* hadn't been going well, and now this? The effect that Moosey's absence had on these kids, especially the sensitive ones . . . it was a last-straw kind of thing. Some of them wanted to go home, and expressed it in no uncertain terms. No one signed up for the Tailfeather Talent show, which is normally a big hit. And our camp songs, I mean, you could forget about it. Frogs eating marbles. It was worrisome. We didn't know how to fix it, all these mopey campers, but *something* had to be done.

I think it was Scott, one of our senior counselors, who came up with the idea. Moosey was missing, yes, and that was sad and infuriating, but maybe there was an opportunity here to, you know, harness some enthusiasm for Camp Winnesaka.

I called an emergency Tribal Meeting in the Chow Hut and told the campers that today was a grave day at Camp Winnesaka. One that shouldn't be taken lightly. A day we shouldn't forget. Some of the campers were crying. I was wearing my ceremonial button blanket and standing below the spot where Moosey'd always hung. I asked them if they had faith in me as Head Eagle. They nodded. I told them that Moosey *was* Camp Winnesaka. And that there are people who are jealous of us. And resentful of all the fun we have here. People who would rather . . . I looked at Eric, the cook, who nodded, and I said, And those people are the art fags across the lake at Camp Chickapony.

Camp Chickapony had nicer brochures than we did. They had a pool.

They said, What are art fags? I said, You don't want to know. Chadwick Thoroughgood raised his hand and said, What now? I said we had to stand up for ourselves. What would the Elders, who are watching us right now, have done in this situation? We had to get Moosey back.

There was a brief moment of . . . I don't know what it was. I could hear kids sniffling. I pulled my button blanket over my head and then flapped my arms to simulate the flight of an eagle and said, We have to get Moosey *back*!

They cheered.

We canceled Crafts and Activity Time to let the campers marinate on what was expected of them. We didn't know, necessarily, where Moosey was, but he certainly wasn't here, and Chickapony seemed like a good place to start. And then Jim, one of our junior counselors, came bursting through the door, dripping wet, and made the announcement that he'd just been at Camp Chickapony, and that they did indeed have Moosey, hanging in their refectory. Upside down. With a cardboard thought bubble taped to one of his antlers. That said "I suck."

I should've—I mean, he smelled like perfume and body odor: I had my doubts he'd actually *seen* Moosey. But skepticism isn't one of the virtues we try to instill in our campers here at Winnesaka. Skepticism is like a gateway drug to more destructive impulses, like cynicism. And who wants to sign their kids up for a summer of *that*?

We stormed Chickapony at night. I figured even if the kids didn't find Moosey, at least it would get their spirits up. Get their blood flowing in the right direction. Generate a little common feeling among the campers for Winnesaka, and we could go from there.

But there were problems. It was an amphibious operation and this wasn't the most athletic or boat-smart bunch we've had at Winnesaka. Our first raid ended—I mean, we were trying to get across the lake, but they didn't even *get* to Chickapony. Jimmy Osteo bumped Randal Jenkins who was holding one of the bow lines, and he dropped it into the water. Tony Rademaker heaved his not-unsubstantial weight to port and bent an oarlock while trying to steady himself. Byron McKinstry said he couldn't see through the masks we'd given them. Then there were the wooden rowboats. They'd always been tipsy, which was the reason we didn't use them much. The paddleboats were fine, they were made of plastic, but they weren't large enough for our purposes. So that, you know, that's why we used the wooden ones. And since we'd sold most of our life jackets to Camp Niateano a couple of summers ago . . . I guess we thought we wouldn't need them. I don't know. So in terms of preparation . . . I mean, it's easy to say always be prepared, but when something needs to be done urgently sometimes you have to go with what you've got and figure the rest out as you go.

A couple of the boats capsized. They were only ten feet

away from the dock. And since Seaweed Sessions had been canceled this year because of cutbacks, there were a few of them who probably couldn't swim as well as they should have. No one died, but there was some floundering. Quinn Kasem ended up drinking half of Lake Oboe, and . . . he's home now. He's doing fine. We just today received a postcard from him, actually. His words bear quoting: "Dear All the Eagles and Papooses at Camp Winnesaka: What . . . fun . . . proud to have . . . been [part of] . . . Camp Winnesaka [where all summers are Indian Summers]."

The campers, I guess, the Quinn incident shook them up a little bit. I reassured them what we were doing was honoring Winnesaka tradition, but some of them were a little slow putting money on the counter for a second raid. I told them that as far as safety goes, how can you feel safe knowing that someone could just creep into camp at any time and steal something as important as Moosey? I mean, what's next? Your sleeping bag?

Thom Sloane raised his hand and asked why we couldn't just *ask* Chickapony to give Moosey back. I told him it didn't work like that. Chickapony campers, they aren't like you and me, I said. You can't just *talk* to them.

Not everyone was convinced, which, I could tell, might complicate things. I was feeling a little nervous about our next raid.

And that's when Ward Hamilton came in. He was—to be honest, I'm not exactly sure what he was doing at Camp Winnesaka. He was good-looking. He had muscles. The rumor was that he'd lost his V-card to his twenty-three-year-old social studies teacher, Miss Robriand. Which would be, you know, certainly within the realm of possibility. This was his first summer here, and he'd already shattered the Archery and Long Toss records, and was in hot pursuit of the Sand Jump record, which I'd set when I was a camper.

We all admired him. He was everything Camp Winnesaka *should've* been. And something about the indignity of losing Moosey, it, I don't know, *touched* him. He took it personally. We didn't even have to ask him to step up. He walked into the Chow Hut in full war paint, gave the Comanche Cry, and led the campers down to the dock like it was something he was born to do.

I addressed them briefly at the water. I put my hand on Ward Hamilton's shoulder and said I was proud of them for avenging this desecration of Camp Winnesaka, and that they should be proud themselves. Plug in and ride the lightning, is what I told them.

The night was very dark, remember. And this was . . . well, they didn't find Moosey. I'm not even sure how far they got. And Ward, it's possible he wasn't wearing a life jacket. Or maybe was wearing it backward. There's a chance that—I mean, it's hard to say what really happened. There were conflicting reports. One kid said he fell in when one of our own boats accidentally nudged his, and he bumped his head on an oar on the way down. Another kid said he'd just jumped into the water. Which doesn't make much sense. I think I'd just like to say that he was admired while he was here, and he was loved. And anytime a camper drowns, it's a tragedy. I know that much.

We had a meeting in the Sacred Circle. I wasn't sure, exactly, what I was going to tell them. I did know that Ward's drowning was . . . well, it had the potential, if handled improperly, to be demoralizing to the campers. Not to mention the Pen Pals. And I think it was Eric who, well, it was his idea, the posters. He had some experience with Photoshop, and he—you've seen them. Ward, in the bow of the rowboat, hoisting Moosey over his head, looking toward the sun which, in turn, is showering him with the golden rays of a Winnesaka summer.

I told them Ward was a hero of no small degree and presented the poster to the Sacred Circle. I said, Never forget. I led them in a moment of silence, and then fixed the poster to the wall of the Chow Hut. We made another one and hung it in the Sandy Can. Grief can be confusing for kids and this . . . well, it put things in perspective, I think I would say. Because Ward didn't just die, alone, in a cold and unbound universe, he died, an honorable Papoose, in an effort to realize all things Winnesaka.

Below the image of Ward, Eric had printed the phrase "Integrity Is Not Born, It Is Learned at Lake Oboe."

Jimmy Donner, who'd been in the boat with Ward, then, this is when he came to us. He was upset. There were tears. I think he'd been binging on chocolate. It was hard to make out exactly what he was saying, but it was something about responsibility. He looked at us and said, Shouldn't there have been . . . ? And Eric just said: Jimmy, don't. We already have another raid under way, and what is finger-pointing going to accomplish? You need to think about what Ward would have done. Would he have fired off accusations? Would he have let doubt win the day?

The next raid was more successful. They didn't find Moosey, but they did come back with one of Chickapony's Sacred Stones. And this, I think in hindsight, we should've been happy with this. But, you see, Moosey was the whole reason for our going over there in the first place. And there was the general feeling around camp that once you start something . . . The ball was rolling, is what I'm trying to say. The campers, they had certain expectations regarding Moosey. Part of it had to do with Ward. Part of it was because one of the things we stress here at Camp Winnesaka is follow-through.

They came back with a boar's head next, which was, I think, sort of like the Moosey of Chickapony. We celebrated in the Chow Hut with extra helpings of Mac and Buffalo. We placed the boar's head near one of the posters of Ward. Things were—well, they were going better than they had in weeks, camper morale–wise. I mean, we hadn't found Moosey yet, and that was a bit of a pebble in our shoe, but we'd been successful in a lot of other ways. We had a boar's head. We had one of their Sacred Stones. Some of the kids even asked me if they could come back next summer, they were having such a good time. A couple of small victories, for them and for me.

But this, then, this is when things sort of got out of control. I'd figured . . . I don't know what I figured. I hadn't really considered . . . I mean, Chickapony is the camp you go to if you can't get *into* Winnesaka. If you look at tradition, that is. I thought they'd appreciate the friendly ribbing and that maybe they'd just send someone over with Moosey, drop him off no-harm-no-foul, and proffer an invitation to their August Potlatch, which we've enjoyed for years. And that would be the end of it. I mean, it wasn't in their interest to begin . . .

The short of it is they hit back, chopping down our totem pole while we were asleep. Dragged it through our crocus patch and softball field and down to the shore, where some boat must've been waiting.

It's hard to explain things to kids. Sometimes you say the right thing, but you could just as easily say the wrong thing. They looked to me, their Head Eagle, imploringly. There was . . . well, they were pretty angry about the totem pole. I was angry about the totem pole. It had been around longer than Moosey, and had been carved by a guy who wasn't alive anymore. Taking that totem pole, it was the height of disrespect. And what are you going to do, drop your kid off at a camp that doesn't have a totem pole?

That night, Eric and Scott came to me and said this back-and-forth needed to stop. Any other year, when we weren't crunched on our numbers, when enrollment wasn't down, maybe it'd be fine. But this year? Tit for tat was unacceptable. And anything short of a decisive and resounding Winnesaka victory was, frankly, untenable in the long haul. They'd talked it over and were in agreement that we needed to mobilize a little more professionally if we were ever going to find Moosey.

Eric said, "I know this is a camper thing, but . . ." I sighed. I said okay.

The two Chickapony campers they shanghaied . . . it was dark, and maybe they didn't grab the right ones, I don't know. Eric put these orca masks over their heads so they couldn't see and sequestered them in the basement of the Arts and Crafts complex. The idea was that maybe they could tell us about Moosey, and the totem pole, and where we could find them. That was all we wanted. But these kids . . . I think they might have been autistic or something. Normally if you put a camper down there, spin him around a few times, and tell him he'll never see his Pen Pals again, he's giving up family recipes and apologizing for the time he diddled his brother in Grandpa's basement. But these Chickapony kids, nothing. They wouldn't crack. And then, see, it's a bit of a dilemma. Return them to Chickapony, where they will most likely help out with future raids, especially now that they *know* the lay of the land here at Winnesaka, or hang on to them until things blow over?

We didn't have too much time to think about that, though, because the next morning we woke up and the Tribal Thunder Stick was missing. We'd only posted sentries on the dock, it hadn't occurred to us that they might come through the woods, don't ask me why. It wasn't an encouraging development. In response, we had the campers stage another raid, and this time they came back with some more Chickapony kids. We tried everything on them—duct tape, maple syrup, dirty talk—but still, nothing.

At that point, some of the campers began wondering if

we were ever going to find Moosey. They were just sort of questioning things, which is natural, sure, and part of every camper's development, but I mean, why now? I told them, beyond a shadow of a doubt we were going to find Moosey. And the totem pole and the Tribal Thunder Stick. And they needed to have faith in me as Head Eagle. If there's one thing I can't stand it's second-guessing, and I think I'm only human in that respect. The implication is that I don't want every camper to have a Winnesaka summer that, you know, shimmers in memory long after the sun goes down. And that's just not true. You think I don't have your best interest at heart? There's a time and a place for this line of inquiry, and to raise these concerns *now,* when we're already invested . . . I mean, honestly.

It came to me in a dream, I think, what we were doing wrong. We just . . . the thing was that we weren't sending enough campers across the lake on our raids. It was taking us too long to search Chickapony, and now, especially, that we had to get Moosey, the Thunder Stick, *and* our totem pole back, it, well, it just made more sense to have everyone go over at the same time.

We didn't have enough boats, though. And this was a problem. It was Eric's idea, I think, the felling of the Spirit Grove. Sure, those trees had been there forever. And they *were* beautiful. And yes, they did house the Ancestral Shades, at least according to Winnesaka legend. But we needed boats. So I figured what we'd do next summer is make it a Winnesaka priority to have the campers plant saplings. Then chart their growth in the growth charts we could have them make in

Arts and Crafts. It would be a new type of bonding experience, and also one we could put in the brochure. Plus, the campers could now add boatbuilding to their list of Winnesaka Activities Mastered when they went home at the end of the summer. They could add logging too.

Before going on, I'd like to say how much I admire the campers at Winnesaka. I'd like to make that clear. Never have I seen such selfless industry. Such unflagging enthusiasm. Such a unity of purpose. Plus, they really seemed to *enjoy* building the boats. We honored every fallen tree with a shout of "Moosey." I caught Sam Stopwell genuflecting as he passed Ward's poster in the Sandy Can. Flotilla formations were drawn up, *X*'s and *O*'s and arrows drawn in the sand. Our campers were campers again. Or maybe for the first time. And . . . well, there's just no substitute for the feeling that gives you as Head Eagle.

They piled into the boats. They were canoes, actually, and we'd painted them to look like tiger sharks and killer whales. I stood on the dock, steadying keels, letting each camper know how important he was to Winnesaka. And to me. I told them we are given few opportunities to shine in this life, and that this was probably one of those opportunities. They began paddling. Fifty yards from shore, one of the kids, Tony Jameson, turned to wave at me.

Well, if I knew then what I know now about the trees, that the reason it was called the Spirit Grove was because all the trees were pretty much rotten and that, you know, even just one rotten plank can seriously affect flotation, things might have turned out differently, sure. I would like to have antici-pated that. It would've been nice if someone had pointed that out. It also would've been nice if the life jackets we did have came with better instructions, and if they were going to be the kind that flip you on your back that they would've said as much. Or at least have been manufactured in such a way that it was impossible to fasten them on backward. But you're not given a crystal ball when you're hired as Head Eagle. I'm not a soothsayer. We're given a budget each summer, and the question is always, do you sink it all into new boats and better life jackets, or do you use it for other things, like sturdy bunk beds, or a new chef? I mean, especially now that we have to have a vegetarian option at every meal. Problems come up, and you solve them as best you can, is what I'm trying to say.

We fished the stronger swimmers, the ones who made it back to the dock, out of the water with pike poles. Eric went to fire up the whaler, but the pull cord had snapped last summer and hadn't been fixed.

Obviously, parents were upset. The phone was pretty much ringing off the hook until we disconnected it. I drafted a letter, which told them that with every death of a camper I, as Head Eagle, die a thousand little deaths myself. Clearly, I wouldn't have sent them if I—I'm paraphrasing here, but it's not the *how*, which, yes, the how was sinking boats and a life jacket shortage, or malfunctioning, it's the *why*. You have to keep the why in mind. And these campers, they died to protect the integrity of Camp Winnesaka for the Papooses still here, and, not to mention, for the generations to come. To call it negligence . . . well, that doesn't really get to the heart of the matter. And it's undermining, not to mention, demoralizing, for the campers who behaved, and were *continuing* to behave, admirably in the service of preserving all things Winnesaka. To sow seeds of doubt in young hearts, I'd say that's unforgivable. The world has enough of that as it is.

We had a ceremony. Of course we had a ceremony. Eric went out of his way to make sure the bonfire didn't get out of control. There was some drumming, and some dancing. The campers read poems to help usher the spirits of their bunk mates safely to the other side, where their spirits could watch from the tops of the rustling trees to see they had not passed over in vain. Which they had not. Because two days later we commenced our Night Owl Rocket Campaign.

It was part of a larger plan to—I mean, we sort of figured this had gone on long enough. We'd all pretty much had it, at this point, with the pussy-foot approach, which was getting us nowhere. Moosey was still missing. We'd lost campers. It was just . . . the feeling was that you can push Winnesaka around only so far. Ronald Beltry, a camper here, wanted to be an astronaut and he knew about fuel cutoff and trajectory, and Todd Splendo, who'd been in juvie, or something, before coming to Winnesaka, he knew a little about gasoline incendiaries. There was the issue of converting our model AO-562 GI Parachute rockets into usable ballistics, but that only took a couple of hours. I mean, besides Jamie Wilson, who, I guess, when he was siphoning gas from one of the Condor Transports, didn't know enough to take his mouth off the hose, or didn't do it quick enough, or just swallowed on reflex maybe, it was a pretty smooth operation to get these rockets up and ready to fire.

We used a wagon to get the rockets down to their launching pads on the beach. After everything was set, I called the campers to me. I told them that there are days, and there are *days*. And this, well, this was one of those days. Honor Ward Hamilton, I said, who would be proud of you, and all the other Papooses who have crossed over in the name of making Winnesaka the safest and most admired camp on Lake Oboe. I told them that people would always be jealous of the fact that they were Winnesaka campers, and that it was a burden they should carry proudly. I looked at them, looking at me. Every pore and follicle in every camper's face appeared to me a tableau of courage. Do not be diminished, I told them.

We fired the rockets. It looked like—well, like nothing *I'd* ever seen. But it reminded me of a legend we tell the campers on orientation night about Chief Winnesaka, who, one day, in his infinite wisdom, realized that what was missing from this forest-world of injustice was light. And so he appealed to the heavens, and said, Let my brothers have light, so that they too can see the beauty of the pinecone and the crystalline simplicity of a swamp frond collecting a drop of rainwater. Let light break through this redwood canopy to mottle the earth so the flowers can bloom and grow and deliver their sweet pollen to the bumblebee. And the heavens, ever mindful, opened in benevolence. The rockets, at their apex, went silent, and forgive me but I feel it's only appropriate to say that at that moment I felt someone standing beside me, a warm and tacit companion, whose nod of approval was small enough to fill eternity.

And I guess it was then that Eric pulled me aside and said he had something I needed to see. I told him it wasn't a good time, the second brigade was readying their rockets and needed a pep talk, and—

He insisted.

He led me through Spirit Grove to the Hondo Lodge. He was sweating a little bit. He was dancing back and forth on his toes and finally I said What? And he said, Well, and then opened this door marked CUSTODIAN, and sitting there, among some life jackets I didn't even know we had, was Moosey.

It was kind of an Oh Shit moment.

Eric said, Oh shit, and I said, Oh. Shit.

It's hard to explain how it—I mean, there are times in every Head Eagle's tenure when he's given a test. And something told me that this was probably one of those times. I knew the impact this revelation could have on things and I didn't like it. I mean, the whole summer, down the drain. That's what's at stake here.

But beyond that, even. Without Winnesaka, would I have ever learned the difference between a red-tailed skooker and a split-wing skooker? And appreciated the value of that difference? Would I have ever canoed across a moonlit lake to put my hands up Sarah Soleil's shirt and rub her pillows after Lights-Out? At the age of fourteen? Would I have ever known countless cookouts? Sing-alongs? Bunk Prank Day? Would I have ever grown up to become Head Eagle, presiding like a benevolent, but firm, older brother to the kids here at Camp? Would my life even have remotely resembled the one I have now? All of that was going through my head. But also going through my head was another question, which was: why is this something that I have to deal with?

And I suppose it was then that Eric turned and said he'd thought it over and come up with a solution. We didn't have to say anything. I didn't respond right away. But it was then, I suppose, that I began to understand the burden we, as counselors, carried. And me, their leader.

Moosey'd started something, sure, but this thing now, it was *bigger* than Moosey. And the campers, they were really having *fun* looking for him. They had come to think of their time here in really specific terms. And if we told them that Moosey hadn't ever been at Chickapony, but had been here, in this janitorial closet, all along?

I guess I would argue that it's selfish, to shatter belief like that. People—cynics—will tell you facts are essential. But facts can be misleading. One fact is not the entire story. And they are downright destructive if you want to get anything done.

Safeguarding Winnesaka, that's my entire job. In perpetuity. If I perceive a threat to camp life, it's my responsibility to address it swiftly and in no uncertain terms. Those art fags at Chickapony, they *did* steal our totem pole and our Tribal Thunder Stick. And, if you think about it, they *were* the reason we didn't have a Spirit Grove anymore. Or Ward Hamilton. Not to mention the other campers.

Eric looked at me. I nodded. We leaned down, put our hands on Moosey, and lifted him off the floor. He was lighter than I'd expected. His expression was unreadable.

We carried him through the meadow, past the gully ferns. Buried him near the Outer Teepees in a patch of brambles.

As we tamped down the soil we could hear the second wave of rockets whistling their ascent. The sun was out. Eric, he flipped open his Swiss Army knife and made a small cut on his thumb. He handed it to me and I did the same. Then we pressed thumbs together. As we walked through the Clover Grove, Lake Oboe came into view, calm and welcoming. On the beach, our campers were dancing around in circles, holding hands like the small children they were, and singing.

the *saint anna*

I n the middle of an endless Arctic night, miles from land, we wake to yelling. "Who's peeing on me?" Vlad is shouting.

"Accident, accident," Dmitri is saying, backing away with his palms up, fly still unbuttoned.

Vlad is standing now, doing a little dance to shake off. "Do you have eyes or just an asshole? The bucket's behind you."

Dmitri looks. Sure enough. "I couldn't see," he says. "I'm *sorry.*"

We are sailors aboard the *Saint Anna,* now in our second ice-bound winter. There are twenty-five of us and we lie like pickled herring in a packed hold, breathing stale air, huddling for warmth, hats on, hands in our armpits, waiting, waiting,

waiting. In an aft cabin our captain Brusilov sleeps in comfort with his niece, Yerminiya Zhdanko, dreaming, no doubt, of the walrus and polar bear we have yet to hunt and the route we have yet to map. We are somewhere in the Kara Sea, locked in an endless sheet of ice, 2,400 miles north of where we should be. Against our wishes we are moving with the ice pack toward the Pole. Land has not been spotted for thirteen months.

We are the forgotten, the unfortunates. Dominoes in a rucksack. Dots on a floe. On all sides we are surrounded by an expanse that cracks and groans according to pressure and accident. Below deck the darkness is complete. Spirits are low. Expectations? You're talking to the wrong crowd. We would think ourselves already ghosts except for the misery of human necessity. What I mean by that: we pee and shit in the subzero, eat to prove we're alive, then sleep and wake to do it all over again.

"Ice-ho," Dmitri says, from inside his sleep-sack.

"Ice-ho," is the response.

My name is Piotr Bayev, and at nineteen I am the youngest aboard. I sleep as far away from the bucket as possible, surrounded by Bolsheviks, Mensheviks, atheists, agnostics, harpooners, navigators, profiteers, carpenters, and criminals. We're marginal seamen, peasants in sailor hats. Men who under *normal* conditions do not get along. Disagreements flash up hourly but our invective is muted, our politics halfhearted. What's the point? Are the twenty-five of us going to solve Russia's problems? We can't even navigate a lead in the ice without someone falling in. We're concerned only with outlasting the ice. Russia can do what she wants while we're away.

The *Saint Anna* is a British-built, gaff-rigged schooner, and we sail under official capacity, sponsored by Nicholas himself. The success of our voyage will be judged on two counts: how thoroughly we are able to explore and map the Northern Sea Route, that hazy passage from Atlantic to Pacific; and the split profits from the hunting expeditions conducted along the way. We hit ice and found early encasement at the hands of our captain, Georgi Brusilov, and as a result have neither mapped nor shot. But Brusilov's an optimist, unburdened by the little things. The kind of czarist who considers our recent war with the Japanese a moderate, if not striking, success. The kind of captain who packs twenty-four months' worth of dried fruit and biscuits for a planned sixteen-month voyage but stocks fuel according to favorable winds. We shoot him looks and he swivels to see who's behind him, as if we might blame someone else for what's happening. We are nowhere now but every day he writes in the log for hours, as if what we're currently undergoing is momentous. As if history will bear us out.

"History might bear *him* out," Yevgeni says. "I should keep a log. 'December 15, 1915: Today I drank some tea. Today I choked myself on a biscuit. Today I went above deck and was surprised to see the ice not moving faster.'"

"Don't forget to write down you're an idiot," Albanov says. "And that we're waiting to freeze to death and all you do is complain."

The temperature outside, when it is clear, is consistently thirty degrees below zero, the kind of cold that fuses teeth together. The wind is cruel and slingshots over the ice like a fury, whistling rigging, snapping stays. From below it sounds like small-arms fire; on deck it's huge oaks cracking.

We've boarded up all hatches and portholes to buffet the cold. We squeeze in, two per sleep-sack, and it doesn't help much. Some of us move in and out of illness. Others simply refuse to rise from their beds, even when Yerminia Zhdanko pleads with them in warm tones.

"It would be good for you to move," she says.

"Why?" is the normal, blanket-muffled response.

Her usual diagnosis is homesickness. That and the fact that we have nothing to do all day except think of the ice. "What are *you* thinking about?" Dmitri asks her from his bed.

We wait for an answer. Dmitri folds his arms. "You can get back to me," he says.

We've put Yerminia Zhdanko's age at twenty. She has a round face and thin arms. Nice breasts, which are most of the time hidden by heavy woolen shawls. The skin on the inside of her forearm, glimpsed at intervals as she fusses about, taking our temperatures, is the color of milk. The logic of her being aboard escapes everyone.

"Think of her as our nurse," Brusilov has said. "Or don't think of her at all."

"Right," Vlad said, when he had gone. "Don't think of her. Easy."

Topsides, snowdrifts slope gently from the ship's rail to

the ice. Accumulation blankets the deck, deep enough in places to tunnel through. Our bowsprit is an enormous, improbably levered icicle that points north toward more whiteness. Fog hangs like cotton in the air for days at a time.

We joke over biscuits that if there were birds in the sky even they wouldn't be able to distinguish the *Saint Anna* from the floes, though with our luck it's probable they would nonchalantly circle and shit a bull's-eye.

"How is that different from your life ashore?" Brusilov snaps.

"Ashore," Dmitri says, "we'd have vodka." The word itself gets a round of applause.

We flesh out scenarios: the ice will either crush or release us, depending on the current; either we will starve to death or we won't. Twenty-five minds and that's about as creative as we get. We've been in the floes for a year and a half. How do you reckon with something millennia in the making? We loathe our astounding inertia. We despise the shivering spectacle we've become. Every day we drift farther north with the ice pack, but the feeling is not that we're moving but that the rest of the world, and Russia, have turned and are drifting slowly away.

Waiting for me in a less frozen part of the world, St. Petersburg—a city with its own problems—are my parents and sister. A tiny house in a blackened part of the capitol district. Like many families ours was unlucky. We queued for bread and compared stories: bad food, not enough food, no food. I had five sisters, four of them dead before adolescence. My older brother, a droshky driver, was killed when his horse kicked him in the head, caving his skull in front of the Mariinsky Palace. His fare, whoever it was, left him in the road to find other transportation. No one told us for days. When my mother finally heard she stopped talking and spent a full week at the stove, stirring vegetable broth into whirlpools. My father stayed at work or attended basement meetings through the night. My sister and I entertained ourselves by seeing who could go unnoticed the longest.

I left home because I couldn't understand the politics that kept my father hopeful. Because he is a Bolshevik I was a Bolshevik, but where had it gotten us? It had gotten us nowhere. He spouted rhetoric and took pride in our immobility. He read *Proletarii* and nodded in agreement. We are the chosen class. It will be manifest. Just look at our sacrifice! How can that not be rewarded? Meanwhile he was being ground away by labor as the party fought with itself accomplishing nothing.

Of course he didn't understand why I was leaving. I told him it was because much happens to a man while he's away. He said: A person like you, a ship will kill you. I knew what he meant. Compared with my brother, I had no personality: no life experience, no opinions about anything, not even two thoughts to rub together. We'll see, I told him. He told me a real worker would never leave. I shrugged. What was I going to do, point out his haplessness? Even the leaders of the party had the good sense to decamp to hotels in Paris; even *they* didn't want to be here. He told me if you don't stand for something you stand for nothing. I shrugged again. The look he gave me went so far beyond disappointment I considered staying. "You are not your brother," he said, finally. "Your brother would not have gone."

"And where is he?" I said, and braced myself.

I left the next morning without saying good-bye.

I found the *Saint Anna* in February. I climbed aboard and was officially added to the ledger. My first two months at sea I managed to fool no one into thinking I belonged. Within an hour of embarking, I saluted the cook twice. I stood in contemplation when told to help the second mate with the foresail halyard. I fouled rigging. One morning, when I was helping Dmitri with the sounding cable, he told me my lack of competence was, at this point, bewildering.

"Wasn't there some kind of test?" he said.

I mentioned my willingness to learn.

"You mean your willingness to do what you're told," he said.

Brusilov had been in such a hurry to disembark he'd all but waved me aboard. "Have you been at sea before?" he'd said. I nodded. "Can you lift that box?" I'd lifted it. "We leave tomorrow."

The first leg—from St. Petersburg to Aleksandrovsk—took six months, one longer than expected. We ported in August and waited for additional crew to arrive. They never did.

Brusilov paced the deck for days until deciding to go on without them. "And she's staying?" Vlad said, pointing at Yerminia Zhdanko.

"She's staying," Brusilov said.

Yevgeni gripped the rail. "I thought she was sightseeing, would eventually tire and leave," he said when Brusilov was below. "This is bad luck. Women on ships."

"You think your luck could get worse?" Dmitri said.

We finally left for Vladivostok on August 28, 1914, so late in the summer it was almost guaranteed we'd get locked in ice. Within two months the leads became too narrow to navigate and we stopped sending men to the crow's nest to freeze in the wind. Gazing out at the frozen Kara Sea, Brusilov absentmindedly chipped ice from the gunwale and proclaimed that this was as expected, and that we would be disgorged without doubt in the April thaw to continue our journey. The important thing, he said, was to have faith. The sea freezes, it thaws. The trick is patience. At this point, we could still see the Yamal Peninsula, rising darkly over the ice in the distance. Not an inviting piece of land, but it was there, so we had patience.

As we drifted north with the polar currents, we watched the peninsula recede until finally we saw nothing but white in all directions. In December, the leads disappeared as if stitched together, and we watched as floes grew into ranges, mountains proclaiming our solitude. It's one thing to know you're at the mercy of something larger than yourself. It's another to see it. Brusilov greeted our looks with a nod, as if to say Yes, but what can you do? Yerminia Zhdanko, on deck, clung to him like a life preserver and took in her surroundings. The ice. Us.

"Bundle up," Vlad said.

April came and we failed to disgorge.

It is January now, 1916. A New Year's celebration—Brusilov's idea—was subdued. We boiled tea with dried cherries and toasted our continuing good fortune. Someone hoisted a cup and requested that we be forever locked together. Vlad explained to him that there are things you can kid about, and things you can't.

It has fallen to me and Yuri to check the contact points where the ice meets the hull. Every day we lower ourselves down from the rail to make our inspection. We look for fissures. We measure drift. Where we can see wood we check alignment. We submit our daily report to Brusilov in writing, which for the last three months has consisted of one word: *same*.

"What's the point?" Yuri said one day when handing it over.

Brusilov didn't look up from his desk. "The point is I told you to do it."

"Bureaucrat," Yuri hissed as we left the cabin.

We've moved through every possible state of mind. Patience was supplanted with panic, which was replaced by a dull boredom that has mitigated the fear. Yevgeni whittles figurines and arranges them on the bulkhead. Vlad practices knots. We've played poker until everyone but Yuri is in unimaginable debt. There are moments of dread. Regret. Listless fatalism. But only Albanov, our navigator, is constantly riled up, telling us we don't deserve to be locked in ice. His murmuring has grown louder over the last few weeks. We are huddled in the galley when he starts in again, in a low whisper, making it known that he's never seen such idiocy aboard a ship, and that someone needs to be blamed and punished. That Brusilov's thorough incompetence needs to be folded back on him.

"What good would that do?" Dmitri says. "Tell me what that would change. Once we're in charge of the ship the ice will just open up?"

"So you're just going to allow this to happen to you?" Albanov says. "You're going to let him take you quietly to your death? We've drifted two thousand miles."

Vlad's near the stove, boiling tea. "Your point?" he says.

Those of us listening shift uncomfortably. It's a familiar conversation. "The happy ignorance of the indifferent," Albanov says to us. "Have you always been like this?" We shrug. "*Happy?*" someone says.

In early January Brusilov takes sick and retreats to his cabin with his niece. She tends to him, boiling tea and bringing him meals. She towels his forehead and locks herself in. None of us have touched a woman since embarking, and we watch the cabin door with an envy that borders on insanity.

"Why lock the door?" Yevgeni says.

"Wouldn't you?" Dmitri says. There's laughter.

"Look at little Piotr," Yuri says. "He's blushing."

Everyone looks. "Keep your hands where we can see them," Vlad says. "Just because *she* can't see you . . ."

I try to think of the ice. I tell them I'm not blushing. This makes it worse. "He can *speak*," someone says.

Brusilov is sick for weeks, and in his absence, no one steps on deck for watch, no one makes trips on the ice to look vainly for leads. Yuri and I stop checking the hull. "You can bundle up to see nothing if you like," he says. "I'm not."

Every night we listen to the *Saint Anna* creak her adjustments. Sleep, when it comes, is sudden and short-lived, constantly interrupted in these close quarters by people coming and going, the shoving for position. We count our supplies. We clean our rifles. We recount supplies. We wait. Conversation has halted except for slurs and insults, which are greeted mostly with shrugs. We have no alternate plan. At least when Brusilov was well enough to make the occasional appearance, our sense that someone was running the ship, no matter how poorly, was intact. Now even that has slipped away, and our time is punctuated only by tremendous, distant thunder cracks, ice sheering itself or gathering together according to some glacial movement we cannot fathom.

Cold, hunger, loneliness, claustrophobia, helplessness, uncertainty, isolation: these sensations crash over us like the memory of waves, and the result for me has been an almost complete eradication of identifiable feeling. I have begun to conjure a dull vision of our time on the ice, and come to understand those of us aboard as less a crew made up of individuals than a singular listless entity, the spin-point on a globe. I feel both inside this ship, and outside of myself. We form a collective pulse; we are contained within the *Saint Anna;* we are far from both land and water, and this has become our home. I have tried to explain this to Yuri, but he won't listen. No one will listen. At a certain point it all comes to exhaustion. At a certain point you pray for something to happen, just so something does.

"To tell the truth, I'm surprised no one's dead yet," Pavel, our cook, says one day to no one.

In February, after Brusilov has regained his health, Albanov, our navigator, informs us he is to leave the ship. In April, he will set out on foot over the ice for Franz Josef Land, an archipelago due very far south of our current position. The islands exist but are delineated on our map by a series of dotted lines that, at their best, read as imprecise. Brusilov says he's free to go as is anyone else. We're surprised. The thought strikes us as absurd. The islands are hundreds of miles away, even by the most generous estimation. "You can't just go," Dmitri says.

"The ice is not going to give," Albanov says. "But you can have faith in whatever you wish."

"Islands that may or may not be there?" Dmitri says.

"Hundreds of miles of ice on foot? Dragging heavy sledges over snow boulders? Realizing halfway there just how awful of an idea it was to leave the ship? Not at the top of my list. I can wait things out right here."

Still, the expedition's announcement has brought some energy back to the crew. We clean our quarters, we are up and about. Within a week, thirteen men have decided to go with Albanov, and with Brusilov's blessing, they set about fashioning additional sledges and kayaks. Some of them are carpenters by trade, others just handy. Those of us who are neither are instructed to chop extra parrels from the foremast or pull planks from nonstructural parts of the ship. Though there are twelve of us who view their departure as fevered idiocy, no one stops them. We're happy to have something to do.

The next day, Yevgeni and I follow Yuri down to the ice to survey the contact points. As we check the ship, Yuri finds an indentation in the hull near the stern. There's a moment of panic—if the ship is crushed, we will all be leaving with Albanov—but after an hour of scraping it becomes clear there is no threat of buckling, what we'd seen had just been an illusion formed from the ice patterns on the hull. Yuri is kneeling beside Yevgeni and me and knocks the ice at his feet with his pike. "We're not getting to Vladivostok," he says. "We have nothing in the hold. Why not leave?"

I have no answer. "Because it's *certain* death," Yevgeni finally says, and stands.

In the evening over tea the men take turns reading passages from one of the few books aboard: Fridtjof Nansen's *Fur-*

thest North. Nansen and his ship, the *Fram,* had become frozen in an ice pack after sailing north of Siberia in an attempt to reach the Pole. Undaunted, he set out with dogs and one companion; they reached 86° north, 13°6′ east before the currents pushed them south. Realizing the Pole could not be attained, they turned back for Franz Josef Land, and, having reached the islands, wintered over. In the spring they made their way to Cape Flora, where they were picked up by a passing schooner. Meanwhile, their ship spent a third winter locked in ice and was then disgorged unharmed into the Atlantic, having traversed the entire Arctic Ocean. "A great movement that felt like no movement," one of the crew said later. Even the dogs lived. We cherish the story.

"Hope's where you find it," Albanov says. "Death's a pale horse. That's why you can't see it coming over the ice."

"What is this, the witching hour?" Yevgeni says from across the hold. Albanov snorts.

Gradually a line is drawn. In the main cabin sleep those who have decided to leave; those of us who are staying sleep in the galley, where we take warmth from the stove. The two groups interact as little as possible, and we have stopped helping Albanov with his preparations. Each group is conscious of what abandonment means: they are leaving us to our death, and we are letting them walk to theirs.

Brusilov is unconcerned. On April first, with the *Saint Anna* still firm in the pack, he feigns surprise to find Albanov still aboard. "I thought you were taking half my crew and leaving to waltz across the ice," he says.

Albanov spits. "Your insouciance is high comedy," he says.

"As is your surprise at finding ice in the Arctic," Brusilov says, before returning to his cabin.

Ten days later, two sledges are loaded with 1,200 pounds of supplies. They take rifles and a shotgun, sleep-sacks, four tents, canned meat and biscuits. Brusilov has kept a log of everything loaned to his former navigator and has made clear that it's to be returned upon their rescue from Cape Flora. Albanov makes no indication he's heard.

There is a small gathering on the ice to see them off. Brusilov remains in his cabin. We help them check the sledges and then they take up the harnesses, seven men per sledge, and begin their journey. We help push for the first thirty feet and then wish them well. After ten paces or so, Albanov turns and drops his harness. The speech he's clearly rehearsed begins like this—"To those of you remaining aboard the *Saint Anna*"—and ends like this: "Never before have I seen such a lazy acceptance of one's own demise. Russia mourns her sons and how they conduct themselves."

We're taken aback. Yevgeni tells him to enjoy being frozen while searching for his islands. Dmitri reminds them to use salt and to think of rabbit when they finally resort to eating each other. We part ways.

Vlad and I stand on deck, watching the fourteen of them make incremental progress to the south. The latest estimation places Franz Josef Land at 235 miles away. The floes stretch like negative space continents on the map. The first night, we can see their tents on the ice from where we stand at the rail, but after three days we see no trace of them. "Lunatics," Vlad says. "Think of those tents."

"Think of *this* tent," Yevgeni says. But we've made our choice. We are here, now, aboard the ship, and we will see what comes.

What does come: in May, readings place us farther north than expected. We express our anxiety by burrowing in our sleep-sacks. If there's nothing to do, we stay put. If there is something to do, we are petty in remembering past work, and refuse to do more than our share. We turn on each other for imagined slights. If asked to move, we grumble about it, or pretend to sleep.

"What's the matter with you people?" Brusilov says. He's come into the main cabin, and is holding a stay that's snapped in the wind. "You going for the If-I-Don't-See-It-It-Doesn't-Exist approach?"

"Does anybody else hear something?" Yevgeni says. "I swear I'm hearing something."

On a certain day a little later, Yerminia Zhdanko ventures into the galley to boil water and Pavel is up like a flash, asking why she can't wait for tea like everyone else. She looks shocked and suddenly ashamed. Dmitri chimes in by telling her to drink as much as possible because who cares. Pavel turns and asks if the tea has Dmitri written on it, at which point Dmitri stands and Yerminia Zhdanko juts her arms between them. "Stop," she says. "Stop. It's not for me. It's for Eugene. He's sick."

Pavel stammers a response that gets caught in his throat.

"Pavel, you see what kind of person you are?" Dmitri says, suddenly proud of himself.

Yerminia Zhdanko makes the tea. Those of us near the galley watch for a glimpse of unexpected skin and are once again disappointed. "I'm trying to help," she says. "He's sick," she says again as she carries the tea from the galley, like there is nothing in this world that could make her understand us.

A month passes with no change. We've augered in. The days wash over us, we care without caring, but then: leads are spotted, breaks in the ice, some distance to the east. It's Vlad who sees them, and sends word below. We are up in a hurry. Dmitri jogs the gangway, his eyes on the horizon. Yevgeni hogs the telescope. We jostle for the best view.

"Are they anywhere else?" someone says.

We crane around. "No, just to the east," Dmitri says. "But there they are."

Relief is palpable. "Are you wetting yourself yet?" Vlad asks Pavel.

"It's within the realm of possibility," Pavel says.

Ignore a problem long enough and it solves itself. Hole up in the wind and the storm will blow over you. I think of Yuri, somewhere out there, on foot in the frigid expanse, hulking his sledge up one ridge and then down another, his goggles frozen, fingers black and dying. We were right to stay. In all likelihood, everyone who left the ship has perished. It is early for hunting—the polar bear are still in hibernation—but it's agreed that, if there are seals, it would do everyone well to have some fresh meat. Dmitri and I elect to go, along with Vlad, Pavel, Batyir, and Yevgeni; it will be a hunting party of six, half the remaining crew.

We set off the next morning on skis, rifles slung over our backs, empty sledge in tow. I am, unsurprisingly, the slowest. Dmitri, at first, waits for me but soon tires of it and moves ahead to join the others.

The leads are farther away than they appeared, and we cannot see them from the ice. At noon there is still no sight of them and there is talk of returning, but we press on, due east, following the compass. The *Saint Anna* recedes until only her two masts are visible, dark against the sky. Then they disappear from sight. Eventually we find a lead and track it east. After two miles it opens into a polynya, a wide hole in the ice through which we can spot the sea. We keep going until the solid ice gives way to grease ice, which won't support our weight, and stop.

After a year it is overwhelming to see water, and there is the sudden realization that it is everywhere under us. "I had, I think, forgotten," Dmitri says. No one responds. The polynya is roughly half-a-mile around. The water is black against the ice, and calm. We stand still long enough to notice a small swell, the seawater lapping gently against the surface ice around the perimeter. It sounds like sand being raked. We had come to understand the ice as an immovable fact of our lives—something that could not be negotiated with, whose endlessness would prove our undoing. But in fact here we were, at its end.

We take off our skis. There are no seals anywhere in sight. "But who cares for seals?" Batyir says. "Look at this miracle." We look at the miracle. The polynya will open wider and wider, fattening the leads until the floes drift apart and we're released to drift in the current, catch the wind, and return home. We remain at the edge of the polynya for an hour without talking until Vlad checks the sun and it's decided we should return to the ship. And it's when we're restrapping our skis that the surface of the water suddenly churns in disarray. We swivel in time to see seals beating it out of the water onto the grease ice. There must be hundreds of them; the sound of their emergence is deafening. A number of them are pups. "Miracle number two," Dmitri says.

In my haste to ready my rifle I forget that one ski is firmly attached to my foot and fall backward, releasing a shot that tufts the ice less than a foot away from Yevgeni.

There is a stunned silence. Everything is halted by the report, even the seals, who seem to forget momentarily what they were doing in the first place. I mumble something about a faulty trigger and force a chuckle. Yevgeni looks murderous. But before his rage can summon any coherence he's interrupted by an even greater disturbance in the polynya, and we watch in astonishment as a great, dark mass slowly breaks the surface of the water, reveals itself, and with a violent hiss, expels a torrent of air. I know it to be a whale, I have seen the creatures from a distance, but up close is something entirely different. The slow beast rolls himself back under, and then the surface is broken by others, an entire pod. The size of each animal is impossible to comprehend. In the air is the smell of their bodies, a fetid warmth; an aliveness that cuts through my head scarf, engulfs my lungs, and brings me to the brink of tears. It's a magnificent spectacle. We count seventeen. Yevgeni, without warning, sends a bullet into the tremendous back of one of the creatures. Its impact is audible, but that is all. "That was less than pointless," Dmitri says. Yevgeni shrugs.

After twenty minutes, the water is still. We regain ourselves and begin to fire at the seals. We're giddy and trigger-happy. It's like shooting balloons tied to a fence. If one is too far out on the grease ice to retrieve, we shoot anyway and leave it.

Our sighting is met onboard with unembarrassed enthusiasm. "A polynya! Whale!" Dmitri says like he's announcing a personal visit from the czar. Eugene turns in slow circles, singing to himself. Yevgeni plants a kiss on Dmitri and earns a punch. Brusilov, all polished buttons, nods smugly and embraces Yerminia Zhdanko. Open water, though we can't see it, is close: otherwise we would not have seen what we saw. It is only a matter of time before the ice gives.

Pavel cooks the seals we have brought back and we glut on second and third portions. The meat is heavy and full of fat. It's the food of kings. Batyir dances his impression of a diving whale. We pour tea and toast the ice. We toast Yerminia Zhdanko. We toast the seals. We toast ourselves and our luck.

"You were almost killed today," Vlad shouts happily at Yevgeni.

Yevgeni pats himself, checking for holes. He raises his glass. "To Piotr: thankfully cross-eyed, the worst shot aboard."

That night we are all afflicted with shits, but it does nothing to dampen the mood. Vlad, hunched over and loosing himself into the bucket, balances a plate of meat on his knees. "A great movement that feels like no movement," he says, grinning and shoving cubes into his mouth.

For the first time in months our hearts pump hope and anticipation.

We spend the next four weeks readying the ship for passage, refastening planks, refitting the masts. From the crow's nest more leads are visible, opening up to the south and east. Those working in the rigging report hourly to those of us on deck. The June sun arches higher now and in the morning smears through the now ever-present mist; the temperature is still below freezing, but the feeling is different. Bear tracks are spotted, and after a brief discussion a group of us leave the ship with rifles. We follow his trail for miles until we lose his track in grease ice. As we return, we see that everyone is standing on deck, watching our sluggish progress. When we're within shouting distance, Dmitri asks what everyone is looking at.

There is no reply at first. Then, a female voice comes over the ice. "Batyir is dead."

"What do you mean?" Vlad shouts.

"What do you *think* she means?" Dmitri says.

We climb aboard. They've brought him up from below and laid him on deck. He's partially covered by a blanket, as if someone were halfheartedly concerned about his temperature. Dmitri, rifle still on his shoulder, moves to close Batyir's eyelids, but they've frozen open.

"How long has he been out here?" he says.

"Long enough," is the reply.

Batyir's skin is the same hue as the ice, a chalky noncolor. His cheeks are sunken and he looks as if he might shatter if mishandled. We stand with the others around the corpse, not sure what's required of us. It seems like a misunderstanding of some kind.

"How'd he die?" Vlad says.

"He just died," Eugene says.

"Was he sick?" Dmitri asks Yerminia Zhdanko. Tears have streaked a path from her eyes to her mouth. Her nostrils are pink and raw. She shakes her head. We watch Batyir for movement. His collar flops with the wind but that's all.

Brusilov comes up from below. "What do you guys do," he says. "Drag misfortune around with you? Just wait for it to catch up?"

"We're going to pretend we didn't hear that," Pavel says.

The fact of Batyir's death fills us completely. What a waste, we are thinking. What a specific thing. And how ridiculous to be following a bear over the ice while all of it happened.

It takes eight of us to lift him from the deck to the gunwale, each trying not to touch or look at him. Brusilov, who has insisted the corpse be brought to water and sunk, stays at a distance, his arm around his niece, and watches as we drop Batyir from the gunwale to the ice. His arms loose themselves from the blanket on his descent and bend at strange angles upon impact. We stand looking down, half expecting this to rouse him. "As if this ship weren't cursed enough," Vlad says as we climb over the rail.

On the ice, we strap Batyir to a sledge and the six of us take turns hauling him in twos. With the harness over my shoulder I feel a panic in my chest like I'm being chased. "Pull, damn it," Vlad says through his teeth. It takes us almost twice as long to reach the polynya with the sledge. Once there, we realize that in order to reach open water someone will have to step off the pack ice and venture, with Batyir, onto grease ice. No one volunteers.

"I am ashamed to be on a ship of cowards," Pastiov says, when it's suggested we push Batyir out as far as we can and shoot the ice around him. We shrug, ashamed ourselves. We offer to tie one end of a rope to Pastiov and hold on to the other as insurance. "Ashamed," he says, knotting the line around his waist.

We tip the sledge and bore holes through the bottom to insure its sinking. Pastiov pushes the sledge out on the thin ice, with Dmitri and Vlad holding the rope. It's not easy going. At each of Pastiov's tender steps we expect the ice to open and swallow them both. Finally within reach of the water's edge, Pastiov stands tall. He regards Batyir for a moment, then looks over his shoulder at us. Then he leans down, and with a final shove, sends the sledge over the lip of ice and into the polynya.

Batyir floats.

"For fuck's sake," Dmitri, his hands on the rope, says.

Pastiov turns and nimbly makes his way back to where we're standing. By the time he joins us, Batyir's almost in the center of the polynya, turning in slow circles on the sledge like a signal buoy.

"What is he doing?" Vlad says.

Batyir's arms have come loose again. Then, slowly, he begins to sink. The water laps quietly over his feet, then his chest, then his head. He hovers below the surface for a few seconds, warped and barely visible, a smear of dull color set against the blue-black water. Then he vanishes.

Two months pass, but the leads, if anything, shrink. We watch in disbelief. It's late July, and we've been on the ice for almost two years. Brusilov blames the polar currents. His refrain has lost all meaning. There's no explanation for what's happening to us except that it's happening.

In the spirit of conservation the only source of light below deck comes from a single smudge-pot, powered by a combination of seal fat and engine oil. The smoke and odor it gives off are enough to make us prefer darkness. I smother the pot and Vlad says, "Yevgeni, imagine my relief I can see you no longer."

Yevgeni has four teeth and is shy about his looks. "Imagine mine," he says.

Our food will be gone in four months. Yuri paces the cabin, pounding his fists into the beams. Dmitri hits Pavel after an argument and breaks a rib. He apologizes only after it's pointed out they were arguing the same side. We consider the sledges but a reading puts us 389 miles off of Franz Josef Land. "We missed our chance," Pavel says, holding his sternum.

Out of everyone, Yerminia Zhdanko spends the most time on deck. She stands facing Russia, for hours at a time, like a widow waiting for some lost ship to return. "You understand, of course, that *we* are the lost ship?" Vlad tells her as she makes her way to her quarters. She doesn't answer.

We wonder about Albanov and his group of explorers. We compile a list of notoriously bad captains and post it in the galley. We check our supplies and wonder how we didn't see this coming. Brusilov has stopped writing in his log. "Not many men," he says one day, "have been this far north."

Vlad crumbles a biscuit onto the table. "Why don't you plant a flag," he says without looking up. "And send word to St. Petersburg."

At this Brusilov spits into a handkerchief, folds it, and places it neatly in his pocket. "If you'd left, you all would've died," he says. "You would've been cut in two by this cold. You would've done nothing. Look at you. What have you ever done? We are very far north. I am alive. You are alive. We will disgorge, and we will map the passage. The last thing anyone needs is more dead peasants." He inhales, and fiddles with his belt. Then he says, "You can thank me for your lives at your leisure."

"*Lives?*" Pavel says.

Ten days later, Alexei takes sick. Two days after that, so does Bogdan. They complain of nausea. Their gums turn black and recede. They run fevers, hallucinate, and describe the unpleasantness of what they see. Readings place us at 82°51′ latitude, well above Franz Josef Land, or any other known islands for that matter. We take another, which places us even farther north, and Vlad throws the sextant over starboard. It clatters on the ice but doesn't break. Dmitri climbs over the gunwale, picks it up, and brings it back aboard. He hands it to Vlad, who throws it again. Still, it doesn't break.

A few days later, Alexei dies without a word. His hands are clasped so tightly together it takes two of us to pull them apart. We wrap him in extra sailcloth and drop him over the rail. We scrape at the ice until we have enough snow to cover most of his body and then leave him. It takes Bogdan another day and then he too is wrapped like a mummy and dropped onto the ice. Soon enough he is covered as well. On deck we stand with our hands in our armpits, leaning against the rail, staring down at the two white bumps. It is Vlad who says that after he dies we are under no circumstances to bury him out there on the ice; stuff him in the bow, tuck him aft, but his body is to remain on board until either the ice breaks and he can be given a proper burial or until everyone dies, and then who cares. There is in us a sudden welling of grief. It's like an anchor breaking its cleat. It comes unexpectedly.

The ice remains ice. The wind tugs at our coats and beats at the hatches. We trudge topsides, only to return below with a new gust of despair. These floes, they are older than anything we can imagine. They were never going to open, and we know now, with certainty, that we will die aboard this ship.

This part should not be rushed, but I can think of no other way to say it, and it must be accounted for. It is an afternoon like all the rest when we, the four of us, Vlad, Dmitri, Yevgeni, and myself, open Yerminia Zhdanko's cabin door and pass through together. It's a ceremony, a funeral procession, symbolic of something. At first we are tender, or we tell her we would like to be tender, but then it becomes something else. Dmitri, holding Yerminia Zhdanko's milky wrists, will not look me in the eye, as I did for him. Her tears move sideways off her face and onto the mattress.

We can hear her through the door after we allow her to close it. Low-pitched, guttural sobs. They float through the ship and enfold us. They are beautiful to hear. We listen, exhilarated by the purity of the sound. "This is too much," Pavel says, with his head in his hands. No one answers. Brusilov, wheezing, threatens to shoot Yevgeni. "You will have to shoot all of us," Yevgeni says quietly, an invitation, knowing Brusilov won't.

Two days later we wake to find Yerminia Zhdanko gone. Tracks run north in a perfectly skied line away from the *Saint Anna*. It is amazing how clear they are.

"You've killed her," Brusilov says, barely able to support himself. "She did nothing to you."

"We've been dead for months," Vlad says. "We are at the end of the world. She brought us to life."

What he means is this: we finally have something that is ours. We've given shape to our time on the ice, and if the floes crush us now, at least it's what we've always deserved.

After this there are no days. The *Saint Anna* groans in the ice for who knows how long. The feeling is that time itself has become unmoored. At night I dream I'm a large whale of some kind, swimming in great dives below the ice. In the water I move through slanted columns of light. Above me is the keel of the *Saint Anna*, like a boulder wedged in a snowdrift. Below is an infinite blue darkness. I have reached an understanding with myself: whatever a person is, whatever he possesses that makes him real, after my time on this ship I am the absence of that. I am not specific; I am the opposite of specific. Everything streams through me. I can hear myself yelling, and it is like screaming into a pillow. I have killed a young girl, and I have not been punished for it. Nothing matters. The ice is pushing heavenward, raising up our bow while the stern remains fixed. Our hull timbers are giving. One or two weeks later Vlad dies quietly in his sleep. Yevgeni checks for a pulse, finds none, and proclaims him lucky. Then he stands, and without a word, walks to where Brusilov is sleeping, and kicks him awake. Driving with his knees, he drops his full weight onto Brusilov's chest. We are not far behind. We fall on him and let gravity bring our blows to his body. He limply objects. We stuff a sock in his throat. When my hand connects with his stomach it's like punching water.

We pack a day's worth of biscuits in a knapsack and tell him to walk. We stuff a map into his embroidered trousers, which are loose on his frame. When he is one hundred yards from our now noticeably listing ship Yevgeni shoulders a rifle and squeezes off a shot in his general direction. The sound reverberates off nothing, a bullet fired into cotton. Brusilov takes a few more stumbling steps, and then collapses. We congratulate Yevgeni on his marksmanship.

We tie Vlad to a sledge and lower him to the ice. We are delicate and sincere. We trudge a half-mile south, stop, and lay a pair of skis in a cross on his chest.

It is only on our way back to the *Saint Anna* that we allow ourselves to comment on the fact that around our ship the floes have pressed themselves into jagged ridges, and our masts are pointing well aft. The sun, having witnessed the burial, shines and reflects brilliantly off the encrusted rime on our stays. Our ship, the fixed point in a frozen gyre; collapsing now under the incredible pressure of the ice. We see that the *Saint Anna* will be splintered and swallowed; we see what will happen a month before it does.

And what of us? If we had courage at all, we would wrap

ourselves in blankets and meet the weather with fateful and furrowed expressions. Instead, we methodically empty the hold of all remaining food and fuel. We empty the ship and lay everything on the ice. It takes us two weeks to prepare for our journey. The mapping equipment we leave. The personal effects, we leave. The rifles, tents, biscuits, dried fruit, sleep-sacks, and everything else, we pack into a single sledge that can be pulled across the ice by the six of us, hitching in turns. The *Saint Anna* stands now almost perpendicular to the ice, as if she herself were some great frozen beast breaking the surface of the ocean, lurching up from the deep. Her masts have cracked. Her portholes are frozen shut. We tell ourselves that when stretched so thin, men will shame kindness and become unforgiving. That survival itself is a form of grace. We tell ourselves that just beyond that ridge, south, will be an open channel, an island; that we will be rescued; that lives begin and end every day, and that we, having passed through more than most, are simply about to embark on another.

the broken group

On the fourth day of their time together—their vacation within a vacation, his father called it—Robert let the anchor chain slip through his hands before he'd been able to secure it and it plunged back into the bay. The chain at his feet uncoiled up and over the bow with startling violence as he stood, frozen to the moment, and watched. The sound of the chain paying out was like playing cards on spokes, but deafening. Within five seconds the anchor was back on the sea floor and the chain paid out. "Dumb," he said to himself. In three weeks, he would be twelve years old. "Idiot," he said.

His father came forward from the cockpit and stood beside him. "What happened?" he said. The engine was idling.

"It slipped," Robert said. "I couldn't stop it."

His father kneeled down and ran his hand over the toe-rail. The chain had jumped its track and gouged the wood on its descent. "Jesus," he said, picking at splinters. He looked at his son. "You all right?"

The boy nodded.

"This could've been wrapped around your legs."

"I know," he said. "It wasn't, though."

His father ran his hand one more time over the rail, then stood and grabbed the line. "We'll do it together," he said. The bay was empty. They hauled the anchor and his father went back to the cockpit and put the engine in forward. When Robert was done washing the deck with the pole brush, he sat down next to his father. "I don't want you to worry about that," his father said.

"What's Craig going to say?"

"Craig's just going to be happy to get the boat back."

The boat—*Pamier*—was a Valiant 32 they had borrowed from one of his father's friends; it was a sailboat built for cruising, a solid and friendly vessel. But, as his father had said at the beginning of the trip, this was the ocean, anything could happen. Inattention had consequences at sea, so it was important to be careful. He'd said it in a funny voice, a captain conjured from a long-lost comic book, but he'd also made it known he was serious. When his mother and sister had been with them, they wore life jackets at all times unless safely below deck. They were to keep one hand on the boat when walking bow to stern, no matter how calm the water looked. Still, with all this preparation: the boom had skimmed the top of Robert's head on a violent jibe, drawing blood, and sent everyone into a silent funk. The propane stove whommed upon ignition. His sister, before she and Robert's mother had left, had been terrified of the propeller.

They glided out of their anchorage into the strait, which was calm, and powered for a time in silence. The sun was out and hot and the wind blew divots in the water. They were heading south, back to Seattle. To the east of them was the mainland, tree-thick hills balded at their tops from clear-cutting. To the west, a view of the unbroken ocean. Robert knew his father wanted to sail, but his father remained silent at the helm as the breeze moved across the cockpit.

"Where are we going?" he finally asked.

"You tell me. We've got three islands to choose from." His father spread the chart on the divan and set his binoculars on it for weight. Robert found his notebook and opened it up. He'd been taking notes on their navigation for the last week. He began a new entry with the date: August 14, 1989. They were in the Broken Group, a cluster of islands sprinkled across Barkley Sound, on the west coast of Vancouver Island. His father circled a spot on the chart with his calipers. "Those three."

Robert studied the chart. One of the islands was shaped like a jagged crescent moon. The other had a cove. "Wower," he said.

"Are you looking at this day?" his father said. "Look at this day!"

* * *

They made it to Wower by midday. His father looked at the chart and lowered his speed as they entered the cove. He kept his eyes on the digitized depth reader, whose numbers jumped wildly as they passed over rocks and shoals. Robert stood at the bow, watching the water for rocks and kelp-clumps that could muck up the propeller. "Okay," his father called from the stern, and he dropped the anchor, and his father backed it down.

Theirs was the only boat in the cove, which was unsurprising, given the recent weather. There had been a storm, and it had caught them, unprepared, seven days earlier. Since it had passed, they had seen only a few other vessels trolling in the distance, and they'd grown accustomed to the isolation, reveling in it even. No more crowded anchorages. No more strange voices carrying over the water, puncturing their sleep. No one watching them except for seabirds and the occasional seal. They were far from home. They rose with the light, and the days, to Robert, felt stretched out and long.

When his father cut the engine, Robert felt relief in the silence. The two of them got into the dinghy, and while his father rowed toward shore Robert paid line over the stern. "Life jacket?" his father said.

"I forgot it."

His father looked at him. "This water's fifty degrees," he said.

Robert nodded.

Ashore, they secured the first line to a birch tree and then hopped over the rocks and looped a second stern-tie around a large piece of driftwood his father said must've rolled from a log boom offshore. Maybe on its way from Alaska. It looked like it'd been there for years, sunk deep, near its base, in the sand. Three points of contact, now. Robert could see his father relax. They would not drag anchor. They were secure.

On the way back to the dinghy, Robert caught the toe of his heavy shore boot on the lip of a rock and fell on his hands. Barnacles dug into his palm, but he kept from crying. His father put a hand on his back and led him down to the shore, and the boy put his hands in the salt water until the sting was gone. "Cold, huh?" his father said. Back aboard *Pamier* his father rummaged through a drawer by the stove and came topsides with some Band-Aids.

The stern-ties were perhaps an unnecessary precaution. For the last four days the weather had been beautiful and calm—the barometer had climbed and plateaued, and the voice on the ship-to-shore radio mounted over the instrument panel droned on and on about pleasant conditions. There was no mention of the storm, nothing of the shipwrecks Robert, before going to sleep, imagined. No distress signals. No calls for help.

"How's the hand?" his father said.

"It's okay," he said.

Later that afternoon Robert went by himself in the dinghy to set the crab-trap, and then rowed over to a kelp-bed and leaned over the side with what his father called the look-box: a cylindrical plastic bucket with a Plexiglas bottom. It worked like a reverse periscope, and below the surface of the water

Robert could see starfish, orange and deep purple, some with too many legs to count. He watched an anemone contract its bluish suckers and then release them to wave gently in the current. He'd remembered his life jacket, and it made hunching over the dinghy's side uncomfortable, but that was the deal if he wanted to go rowing by himself: life jacket at all times, and stay within sight of *Pamier*.

Ashore, his father showed him how to fillet the salmon they'd caught the day before, which made him squeamish but also, as he put one gloved hand on the body of the fish and with his other made his first cut, exhilarated. As he felt for the spine with the knife, he remembered how his father had brought the club down on the fish's head, three whacks, until it stopped flipping around and lay in the cockpit, stunned at its own suffocation, its gills clapping open and shut. Robert had never seen his father hit anything, and watching this he'd felt his own weight to be less than the fish's. He had caught it. He had hooked and reeled it in. His father had been at his shoulder, excitedly shouting instructions about line tension and angle, finally grabbing the fish with one hand while the other reached for the club. The wet blows sounded like a cabinet shutting. "That's *your* fish!" his father had said, holding it up for appraisal before dropping it on the deck. Robert had smiled, but then had felt ashamed. He wanted to throw it back, or at least part of him did, but the blood was dark, and its scales, like small mirrors in the sun, had flecked off onto his shoe. It could not be undone.

After they'd collected enough wood for a fire, Robert walked on the beach below the tide line, picking up sand dollars and skipping them back into the water so they wouldn't dry in the sun. He flipped rocks and watched tiny crabs scuttle over one another in the sand. He delicately carried a crab in the basin of his shirt to a tide pool, crouched down, and dropped the crab into a sea anemone, which closed itself around the crab. It looked to him like a hug; a greeting. He didn't know whether or not anemones ate crabs, but eventually the crab stopped moving, and the anemone opened itself again.

They cooked and ate the salmon ashore, and after dinner they sat facing the water as the sun went down. As the light flattened, they saw an eagle, and watched it dive and swoop just beyond *Pamier*. Soon it was dark. When Robert began to get sleepy, he and his father stood and peed on the fire side by side and then his father kicked sand over the remaining embers. On board, they slept in the main cabin, together. It had been this way since his mother and sister had left, the two of them bunking up, and it was a comfort to Robert. He would not have admitted it, would not have said it aloud, but he was unable to sleep in the unfamiliar boat, with its stays and halyards constantly adjusting in the wind, knocking into the mast, without knowing his father was two feet away from him, in a matching and old-smelling sleeping bag.

The storm had come up suddenly, and had been more severe than the man on the weather channel had predicted. When the wind picked up, his father jokingly announced it was time to batten the hatches and get out the board games. "I don't think this is funny, Joshua," his mother had said. His father looked at her and shrugged. He went topsides to check the anchor and returned below to say there was nothing to worry about. Robert's sister was two years younger and scared of the wind. When they were in their sleeping bags in the bow cabin that first night, the cabin the two of them had decided to call "the cave," he'd let her sleep on his bunk between him and the hull.

The next morning a front rolled in, bringing with it a gale-force warning. His parents discussed trying to make it to Ucluelet, but by the time they'd decided to leave, the wind had already arrived, and his father said it was too late. It would be safer to stern-tie to shore and hunker down than to attempt an open-water crossing.

"There are no other boats here," his mother said.

"We'll be fine," his father said.

"You think, or you *know*?"

His father didn't answer but turned to Robert and told him to put on his foul weather gear.

"You must be joking," his mother said. Robert had never seen her so angry. "He's not going out there with you." Outside, through the hatch, it was dark.

"I need someone to help with the stern-tie."

"Well, not him."

Robert already had his slicker, but his mother told him to put it away. "How could you do this to us?" she said to his father, almost under her breath.

"What do you want me to say? I'm sorry."

"You knew it was late in the season to be out here. You

told me." She opened the closet near the galley and pulled out a pair of rain pants and slammed the door shut. "You might have grown up sailing, but no one else here did. You understand? This might not be scary to you. But I'm telling you. This isn't fun for the rest of us."

His father watched her stomp rain boots on. When she stood, he was still watching her.

She turned to Robert and his sister and told them not to worry, and then she climbed topsides after her husband.

The two of them watched the storm and their parents' progress through the oval-shaped cabin windows. The trees onshore whipped and swayed. The rain was coming down sideways and in sheets, and looked at times to be billowing in the wind. He could hear his parents shouting, but it sounded like a combination of directional advice and nonsense.

"What if they don't come back?" his sister said. She was nine and shorter than he was by a foot, with her mother's brown hair.

"That's stupid."

"What if?"

After a while they heard their parents scrambling back aboard and Robert turned to his sister, who was crying, and said, "See?"

That night his sister whimpered until their mother brought her sleeping bag into the forward cabin and slept with the two of them. In the morning the storm seemed to have passed over them at least partially, but the voice on the radio said that in the north, hurricane winds were being reported and an all-craft advisory was issued. They spent the day in the cabin playing cards and board games. When the wind kicked up again, Robert's father went topsides to check the anchor and returned wet and angry. "We're dragging," he said.

"What can we do?" his mother said. It was the first time they'd spoken to each other all day.

"I don't know," he said.

Robert's sister began crying again. "That helps," his father said. "The crying helps."

At some point, Robert fell asleep, and when he woke up he was surprised at how quiet it was in the main cabin. The storm had stopped. Morning light was streaming in through the hatches, which were now open. His father sat at the chart table with the radio on low volume.

"We're taking your mother and sister to Ucluelet," he said. "They'll catch a bus and then a ferry home."

"What about me?"

"I need you," he said. "The boat has to come down. I can't do it by myself. The storm's over. It'll be fun." He stood and stretched. "We can poke around the islands for a few days before heading down. Me and you. It'll be fun. I promise."

It took six hours under power to get to Ucluelet. As they pulled past the breakwater, his sister pointed to the shore abutting the marina, where a number of the boats that had been free anchored were stacked almost on top of each other, as if they'd been swept into a corner by a large broom.

Robert hugged his mother and said good-bye to his sister at the bus station. His sister was crying for no reason. She gave him a drawing of a tree, and he thanked her for it. They waited for the bus to pull out, and then he and his father returned to *Pamier*.

Later, they talked about Robert's mother. "She thinks I put us in danger," his father said. Robert nodded. "I don't know what she told you and your sister. But I want to tell you I didn't do that. She's wrong about that. I was maybe not as careful as I could've been. But look, I got us out of it, right?" Robert nodded again. "No one's hurt." They were playing Rummy-Block on the foldout table in the main cabin. The wick on the kerosene lamp was low, and the light was soft.

"I figure as long as we avoid the pirates, we'll be fine from here on out," his father said. He cocked an eyebrow.

"That's lame, Dad," Robert said, putting his tiles on the board.

"Not true!" his father said. "I heard them, just last night. Rowing around the boat, singing yo-ho-ho. I didn't want to wake you. I didn't want to scare you."

"I wouldn't be scared of *that*."

"Oh yeah, tough guy? What would scare you?"

Robert felt like he'd been kicked, caught by surprise. He wasn't ready for this. He'd thought about it, but thinking wasn't the problem. He wanted to say, being alone. He wanted to say the kids at camp this summer, so sure of themselves, scared him. But he couldn't. What could his father possibly say? These kids, they had hated him for no reason he could think of except that he was there by himself and hadn't, like them, signed up with a group of friends. He wanted to tell his father that when these kids had lured him deep in the woods, and tied him to a tremendous oak and left him, he'd been scared. It wasn't when they were there, though, laughing, and pulling his shoes off, that he'd been truly frightened; that deeper fear had only come after they'd left, and there was almost no sound in any direction, nothing for him to grab onto at all, and he'd understood he was lost. It was an isolation he'd never felt before. When he'd finally untied the knots, it was getting dark, and he still didn't know which direction the camp was; he'd sat at the base of the tree and cried until a counselor had come to find him. He hadn't moved, just like he'd been instructed to do. No one apologized, but he hadn't wanted anyone to apologize. He'd wanted to disappear. He'd wanted to just be blown to the ground and stepped on as if he wasn't there. He'd told no one. Not his father. Not his mother when she came to pick him up at the end of the week. He kept it to himself, hardening his memory of that long afternoon until it was diamond sharp. It had happened to him, and it couldn't be changed.

"Not pirates," Robert said.

His father let him win the game, and then they turned in.

The next day at Wower, Robert woke early. He'd slept in his clothes, which made him aware of his mother's absence and also made him feel older somehow. His father wasn't in the opposite bunk. He went topsides, rubbing the crust from his eyes and squinting at the morning sun. The air smelled fresh. His father sat in the cockpit, reading Louis L'Amour and drinking coffee.

"Want some?" he said. Robert nodded, and his father poured coffee from a thermos into a cup. The cup was made from red plastic, and across the front BOSUN was written in maritime font. His father drank from the FIRST MATE cup. Robert never drank coffee at home, and having it this morning with his father felt like a secret between them. He went below and came back with his own book, a Gary Paulsen novel he'd already read about a young boy surviving alone in the wilderness, and sat next to his father until the sun was high enough that it didn't feel like morning anymore.

When his mother and sister had been aboard the days had been crowded with shore exploration and card games and elaborate hunts for pirate treasure, but the four days with his father had been punctuated only by occasional conversation and eagle spottings. The hours unraveled, and then it was time to eat. Or time to pull up the anchor and brush the deck down. Robert preferred it this way. It wasn't that he didn't miss his mother and sister. It was just different without them. Quieter. Grown-up.

His father stood. "You want to help me wash her down?" he said. Robert shrugged. "Get your stuff, then," his father said.

After he changed his clothes and put on his life jacket, he handed the bucket of soap water to his father, who was sitting in the dinghy, holding on to the toe-rail. Then he turned and climbed backward into the dinghy, searching blindly with his foot for the seat. He felt his father's hand on his back, felt the seat with his toe, and let himself down.

They spent a good half hour washing the port side, his

father inspecting every scratch and wondering aloud if it had been there before the storm. It was hot and his father pulled his shirt over his head and threw it on deck. When they got to the bow, his father told him to sit down and then grabbed ahold of the anchor chain and pulled them under. As they moved under the chain, Robert looked up from the bottom of the dinghy, where he'd been watching sand swish back and forth in an inch of seawater, and toward shore. Standing at the tide line was a man in a red flannel shirt. His arms were crossed, and though he was more than fifty yards away, Robert could feel he was staring at them.

"Dad," he said.

His father turned. At first, the man did nothing. Then his father cupped his hands and said, "Hello?"

The man slowly raised his hand. He was the first person they'd seen in the islands since the storm.

Robert's father stood still in the boat, watching the man. He reached for the toe-rail and missed it, reached again and grabbed it to keep them from drifting.

"Thank God you came!" the man said. He didn't shout. His voice carried over the water. It sounded like his voice was coming from behind them. The man's hair was brown and disheveled. Something about the way he stood struck Robert as odd, as if one leg were longer than the other.

Robert's father looked over his shoulder, scanning the bay to see if he'd missed a boat. He laughed. "We came?"

"I'm wrecked," the man said. "On the other side. Of the island. You're the first boat I've seen."

His father asked him if he was all right. The man said yes.

"Do you have a radio?" his father said. "Did you radio it in?"

The man said nothing. Then he said, "Yes, it's a little frazzled now though. I never got a time, but they said they'd be coming."

"The coast guard?"

"The coast guard."

His father turned and put his hand on the rail and then turned back to the man. "You need help?"

The man dug his boot into the sand. Then he laughed. A rough sound, more like coughing. He kneeled down, picked something out of the sand near his boot, and as he stood, put whatever it was in his shirt pocket. "Clearly," he said.

Robert's father looked at his son, and then back to the man. "Okay," he said. "Hold on. We'll be right there."

His father told Robert to climb aboard and tie the dinghy. Then he heaved himself aboard as well. Robert tried a buoy knot his father taught him, but it didn't take, so he tied a square knot. He looked at the man, who was standing perfectly still, and then followed his father below.

"Are we going?" he said.

His father was looking at the ship-to-shore radio. He sat for a while not saying anything. Then, finally, he told Robert to get some food from the cabinet and put it in a paper bag. He packed some Doritos and crackers. Some cottage cheese. As he was reaching for the soda, his father said, "Sort of came out of nowhere, didn't he?"

Robert nodded. "Maybe we should call someone," he said.

His father didn't respond. Robert looked out one of the cabin windows but couldn't see the man. He went farther stern and looked out another window and then saw the man standing near one of their stern-ties, inspecting it. "Well, let's go," his father said.

Robert sat in the stern of the dinghy as his father rowed toward shore. The dinghy pulled left and every five strokes or so his father glanced over his shoulder and corrected their path with a few port strokes. Robert held the stern line in his lap and practiced tying bowlines so he wouldn't have to look at the man, who was waiting for them on the beach, standing almost perfectly still. When they landed, he made no move to help them.

"Father-son thing, huh?" the man said.

Robert climbed over the bow, and he and his father pulled the boat over the sand until it was above the tide line. They found a rock and looped the bowline around it.

"You got it," the father said.

The man looked at Robert. "I think it's okay to take your life jacket off now," he said. Robert flushed and fumbled the clasps. The life jacket was too big for him and made him feel like a child. He dropped it in the dinghy. "What's your name, my man?" the man said.

Robert looked at his father. "Robert," he said.

The man smiled. "Robert," he said. His eyes were deep brown. His face was like bark. "Robert." He took a breath. "Like the poet."

Robert said nothing.

"Like his uncle," his father said.

"Like, his, uncle," the man said. Then he turned to Robert's father. "You can put the Doritos down. I have food. You get caught in the storm?"

Robert's father set the bag down at his feet. "Yup. We were moored. At Alma Russell, farther in."

"No shit. I know that island."

Robert looked at his father, who was shifting his weight around like he couldn't get comfortable. The man's forearms, crossed on his chest, were gigantic. Robert guessed he was over six feet tall. "Well, didn't that wind come out of nowhere?" he said. "One minute, sky's clear to Japan. Next minute the furies. Least you were in a nice boat, though. Those Valiants. Nice boats."

"We were lucky."

The man ran one of his hands through his hair, got stuck halfway through, and tugged it out. "Well like I said. I got wrecked on the other side here. Just been waiting for someone to swing by. You're the first boat I seen."

"Four days ago?"

"I suppose so. I suppose that's what it would be."

The boy's father looked over his shoulder at *Pamier*. They'd left the hatches open. "We were about to pull anchor," he said. "We're heading south. We could tell someone. Call it in on the radio."

The man shook his head. "I just gotta move some stuff ship to shore, if you know what . . . two people could do the job, easy.

It's a"—the man paused to watch something in the distance—
"portable generator. Some food. That's all. The boat's wedged
on a shoal. Just can't do it by myself. Half an hour, tops."

"We're on a tight schedule."

"Half an hour," the man said. "Tops."

They followed the man up the beach. On this island the woods
hugged the shore and began near the high-tide line where sand
gave way to rock. The trees were dense, their green branches
enormous and windblown. At their base was a thicket of
brush and bushes, grown together and knit closed by years of
weather, a natural wall that appeared impenetrable to Robert.
The man walked quickly until he'd led them above the tide line
and over driftwood. When they got to the edge of the beach he
stopped, turned to Robert's father, and said: Ta-da. The opening into the woods was obscured by dead branches. It was less
than ten feet from where they'd had their fire the night before,
a small, almost invisible, seam in the growth. The man bent
over and picked up a desiccated buoy in their path and hulked
it into the woods before continuing up the dirt trail, motioning
for them to follow.

He led them at a slow pace, stopping now and again to
kick a branch out of their way or sometimes for no reason at
all. They stayed close behind him. Sunlight filtered through
the oak canopy and mottled the ground at their feet. It was at
least ten degrees colder inland. Robert felt like he was now
walking through a Gary Paulsen novel, bushwhacking the wil-

derness. He focused on the man's feet in front of him. His boots were brand-new, barely scuffed. He and his father were both wearing sneakers.

After ten minutes of silent hiking, the man suddenly stopped and turned. He put his hands on his hips and looked at them, as if he were considering something. Then he grabbed Robert's shoulder and said, "If you look up, you can see an eagle's nest."

Startled, Robert stepped back but was held in place. He looked up. He didn't see anything but trees. "Right there," the man said.

"Where?" his father said. He'd been a few feet behind Robert, but moved now, and put his hand on Robert's other shoulder.

"In the trees," the man said, releasing Robert and pointing. "Top of that one, there."

Neither Robert nor his father saw anything that looked like a nest. The man shrugged. "Take my word for it," he said. "Eagle nest."

"Okay," Robert said. "Okay."

The man turned back up the path. "You ever see an eagle catch a salmon?" he said after a few minutes. He seemed interested only in talking to Robert. His father stayed close. He had fallen behind them a number of times as they weaved through the woods, but now he stayed close.

"Yeah," Robert said, even though he hadn't. He'd seen eagles, plenty of them, flying while gripping salmon, but hadn't seen an actual catch.

"Water, then air," the man said. "Imagine it. Just imagine."

"Something else," his father said. "For sure."

On the map, the island hadn't looked large enough for a forest this size. They walked for fifteen more minutes, scrambling over debris felled by the storm, Robert's father helping him by keeping a hand on his back. They walked through ferns and over moss. They passed fishing buoys lodged in the crotches of trees. Robert pointed out to his father what looked like a flannel shirt and a pair of pants draped over a bush, as if hung there to dry. His father nodded, and then looked at it like he was working something around in his head. Finally they broke through the other side into the sun, and Robert was filled with relief. In front of them was a huge cropping of rocks, and below that the water. The beach itself was piled with driftwood, sun-stained logs rolled tightly together like bleachers.

The man turned to them. "Down this way," he said.

"What way?" his father said.

"Around."

His father stood there. "Four days?"

The man looked at him. "About," he said. He pulled himself up to his full height and smiled. "About."

Robert's father was quiet. Then he said, "Let's do this, then. My wife's waiting for us."

"On the boat?" the man said.

"On the boat."

The man laughed, and looked at his shoes and then looked at the sky like he was checking the weather. "No, she's not," he said. His tone was friendly, as if he were kidding an old friend. "Why would you say something like that?"

Robert followed his father, who followed the man over the rocks. They walked with their backs to the forest, moving slowly, the man not looking at them. From behind it looked to Robert like the man was covering his mouth. He picked up his pace, and as they approached the end of the outcropping he was almost at a run. He put some distance between them, then he suddenly stopped and turned. "It's—" He stumbled. "I'm down here," he said. He was pointing, but Robert couldn't see at what.

Robert's father lightly put his hand on the back of his son's neck. "There's no easier way down?" he said.

"Swim," the man said. His eyes were wild. "I swimmed."

Robert noticed the man's mouth was bleeding slightly. The man looked at Robert like he'd just remembered him and smiled. One of his front teeth was smeared brown. He looked like he was trying to keep from laughing. "I swum to be here with you today," he said.

"You all right?" Robert's father said.

The man shrugged and looked over his shoulder at the ocean.

"We're leaving," Robert's father said to his son. Then he turned to the man. "We're leaving now."

"You can't," he said. "I'm just down there."

Robert was aware of something passing between his father

and the man but couldn't place it. His father was kneading his shoulder, pressing him into his body.

"Come down here," the man said. "Two's enough."

"No," his father said. Robert felt his stomach tighten. He was getting dizzy. He thought he might throw up. "We're leaving."

Robert walked quickly with his father behind him toward where they had come out of the woods. "Move," his father said. He was worried they wouldn't be able to see the trail-head, but it was clear, as if everything were pointing them in the right direction. At the edge of the forest he looked back and saw nothing but the windswept shore, debris littering the beach. Seaweed above the tide line, dry and cracked and fly buzzing.

When they were twenty yards up the path his father said, "I need you to run." He said it in an almost unrecognizable register, and it was this that frightened Robert. More than the size of the man. More than his dead tooth. His father's voice. It seemed conjured from the earth, something from the soil.

They ran for what seemed like half an hour but though Robert was exhausted he didn't slow. Twigs snapped across his face. His father's breathing was loud in his ear. He tripped, stood. Tripped again, and felt a sharp pain in his ankle. He made no sound. He told himself that was something he was not going to do. He stood and felt his father's hands on him, felt himself being lifted off the ground. He held tight to his father around his rib cage and his father held tight to him, carrying him down the path. Robert shut his eyes. He pushed one of his ears to his father's chest, and became overwhelmed by the fact of his father's jostling body, cradling his own while careening through growth. He felt his father's breath on the top of his head. He felt his father's beating heart. He felt his father's arms around him, iron and unbending. They were a tree themselves, moving through other trees.

They were pushing the dinghy and had it halfway down to the water when the man came barreling into the sunlight. Robert saw his father reach for the fish club in the bottom of their dinghy, grab it, and turn. The man stopped briefly at the mouth of the trail, snorted, then resumed his charge. Arms outstretched, like wings.

What happened, happened fast. His father's arm arced high, the man never slowed, the club came down with a sound that made Robert's knees go out from under him. The man stepped back once, and then collapsed forward onto Robert's father, bringing them both to the sand. His father exhaled what sounded like an animal whine, untangled himself, and then limply hit the man again with the club, this time on the back of the head. Then again, harder, with a blow that pushed his features into the sand. His father yelled something at the man, or at himself, Robert wasn't sure. The man was motionless now, but his father, half-standing, hit him one more time. And then there was silence. The world had hushed. Robert, on his knees near the dinghy, watched a crab, watched a piece of seaweed, watched the rocks. He did not want to look up. In both hands he had fistfuls of sand. His father took him quickly in his arms and then the two of them pushed the dinghy into the water and began rowing toward *Pamier,* his father grunting with each stroke, Robert in the bow, as far away from his father as possible.

On the boat, they sat in the cockpit. The man, still on the beach, wasn't moving. Someone his size, Robert imagined, would, in a few minutes, rise. But they watched for a few minutes, and nothing.

"Is he dead?" Robert finally asked. He'd searched for and found the fillet knife they'd left in the cockpit and was now holding it in his lap.

"I don't know," his father said. "I don't think so."

Robert wanted to say the man needed help, but was afraid.

"Give me your knife," his father said.

Robert shook his head.

"I need to cut the stern-ties. Please."

Robert handed his father the knife, and he leaned over the stern and began sawing the lines. Then he gave up. "Just untie them," Robert said. His father looked at him and then at the cleats that held the lines, reached down and freed them. They dropped into the water with a tiny splash, and sunk.

On the beach Robert could see the bag of food they'd brought for the man, tipped over, its contents not six feet from him. The orange of the Dorito bag. The soda can catching the light. It looked like the man, carrying a bag of groceries, had suffered a heart attack and fallen. Not in the sand. Not on a desolate beach in the Broken Group on the outside of Vancouver Island. But in an asphalted parking lot, where someone would find him, tell whoever needed to be told, and be on their way.

His father stayed in the cockpit. He did not go below for the radio. He did not reach for his son. He sat perfectly still, watching the beach.

Finally he asked Robert if he was hungry. Robert shook his head. "Thirsty?" he said.

"No."

Then he said, "Your mother loves you very much," and Robert started crying.

The sun was high over the mast, and the dodger didn't provide much shade. Robert's father was sweating when he stood. He looked at the beach and then told Robert he was going.

"Where?"

"I'll be right back," he said. "I'll be right where you can see me, the whole time. In sight of the boat. I'll be back."

"He needs help," Robert said.

His father didn't say anything.

"He needed our help."

His father coughed and then asked him if he remembered how to use the radio. "I'm coming with you," Robert said.

"No."

His father climbed down over the lifeline and into the dinghy. Robert followed him and stood at the rail.

"Do you want the knife?" Robert said.

His father shook his head. "This is not your fault," he said, and then pushed off the boat and began rowing to shore.

"Why can't we just leave him?" Robert said. He knew his father, thirty feet away in the dinghy, could hear him, but there was no response.

From *Pamier,* Robert watched his father beach the dinghy. He stepped onto the sand and, holding the fish club close to his leg, approached the fallen man. Once he stood at the man's side he bent over, as if whispering to him. Then he straightened up. He turned to face the woods, turned again, and lobbed the club underhand toward the dinghy. When he saw Robert watching him he raised one hand in a wave. Robert waved back. Then he saw his father bend over the man, again, put his hands on his shirt, and pull. The man was enormous, and as he watched his father lose his grip, and try again, it seemed to Robert like the man had become lodged in the earth. Eventually he came loose. And Robert watched as his father began to drag the man up the beach, toward the tide line.

It was not easy going. He could hear his father strain with the load, grunts that reached across the water as he jerked and tugged. The man's shirt ripped and his father fell backward. He stood, wiped the back of his pants, and then clasped the man's hands in his and pulled him that way. The toes of the man's boots carved parallel grooves in the wet sand. Behind both of them, the trees loomed motionless, a painting of trees.

Robert saw where his father was going, and wanted to tell him to stop. At the mouth of the woods, his father straightened up, paused for breath; then he bent over, found the man's hands again, and disappeared into the growth. The man's trailing legs jerked incremental progress until he too disappeared into the woods, and then there was silence. Free of the stern-ties, *Pamier* began to drift over her anchor. The wind picked up. Robert thought of his sister, at home, and then thought of the radio. He imagined a distress signal, issuing out from his boat and pulsing under the waves, washing up across the ocean. He imagined someone who looked like his father, but older, removing the receiver and answering. Lighthouses rhythmically sweeping the bay. He unsheathed the fillet knife and lay it across his lap. He listened in their gentle anchorage to the wavelets sucking against the hull, and waited. He promised himself he wouldn't move until he saw what he wanted to see. Someone—perhaps many—would come. They had to.

a mugging

What do we need to know about these people? Her name is Claire; his name is Charles. They are in their early forties, white, both architects—he works downtown, and she works from home, freelance. They've been married twelve years, and their time together has been punctuated by moments of happiness so engulfing that even the major interruptions—the birth of their son, her parents fourth-act divorce, the slow introduction of their own mortality—have been hurtled with the brio of inebriated three-legged racers. They are out walking now. They've just seen a movie neither of them cared for. They are looking forward to getting home. Can you see this particular train coming? Is there anything you or I can do to stop it?

It's ten-thirty now. I feel like there's still time. But there they are, walking toward their car, not listening to me, or to anyone.

Before the attack, they will, the two of them, have been talking about her mother's love life, her mother who is now dating after years of mistaking solitude for happiness, and their plans for the upcoming weekend. Afterward, they will drive home in a silence he will later interpret as quiet accusation and she will interpret as mutual reverence for the fact that they are now both back in the car, moving safely away, doors locked as if muggings had aftershocks like earthquakes. *Just a wallet with the credit cards and a cell phone, it was my husband's wallet, and my purse,* she'll say into the telephone after they've explained to the babysitter why they cannot pay her tonight and have turned on all the lights in the house. *Just,* her husband hisses. He's overheard her from the bathroom where he's leaning over the sink and letting pinkish drool drip from his mouth. He'd been hit hard. No words had been exchanged. Just hit. Bang. He didn't even see the guy who hit him, couldn't have said if he was enormous or small, he could've been the Chrysler Building for all he knew.

In the car, they'd talked about the emergency room—she'd wanted him to go, but he'd said *no* with such quiet force that she didn't argue. It was dark where they'd parked, but soon they joined traffic, other people in their cars, and it was when

THE PERIPATETIC COFFIN

they merged onto the freeway that he'd started crying. She'd pulled onto the shoulder and reached for him, but he'd pushed her away. Harder than he meant to. And then he'd said *just drive*.

Home. The sitter paid and gone. After checking on Sam, their son, happily watching a movie on his own, barely nodding as she asks if he had fun, pushing her away after a few seconds when she comes to hug him on the couch while Charles stays outside the room, she will call to cancel their cards and inquire about any recent charges, and the woman on the other end of the phone will say how sorry she is to hear about things like this. That it happens more than you'd think, meaning not just the losing but the violent taking (she will hear this, for some reason, as "violet talking" and ask the woman to repeat herself). The good news is that the card can be canceled and of course all the charges if there are any will be reversed. In fact, there is a recent charge, the woman says, I'm seeing that. It'll be reversed, don't worry. Where was it? The woman will tell her, it's across town, and Claire, surprised at the calm with which all of this is being handled, will say thank you. Her husband is pacing the kitchen, opening and closing drawers, looking for who knows what, some crackers, she supposes, to go with the whiskey he's poured himself, the alcohol that is making him wince as he slugs it back and sluices it around like mouthwash. His lip is swollen. His eyes are distant but burning, or drowning, she thinks drowning might be a more appropriate description of what his eyes look like, the same eyes she's seen and loved every day for thirteen years, since even before they were married, these eyes that have only looked at her the way they are looking now twice in their life together, which is more like a not-looking, a scanning without seeing, as she tips his head back to get a closer look at his mouth in the light of the kitchen. She's not a doctor, but she knows the hospital isn't going to enter the picture tonight, that all he needs is the ice and alcohol he's already allowing himself, and without thinking she pats his head to indicate she's done with her inspection, a school nurse gesture, a this-gets-better-I-promise, your parents will be here to pick you up soon. As soon as she's done it, there's the hope he'll interpret this as reassurance, but it's dashed by a *goddamn it, Claire.* As if this were a mode of hers, this infantilizing. She reaches for the phone again, this time to call the police, but her husband tells her to put it down, tells her while refilling his glass and then filling one for her *what are we going to say, that some black kid hit me?* and she will say that it wasn't a black kid, that she had seen him and it was a white kid, or a mostly white kid, and that when he had punched her husband she was so scared that she just held out her purse in front of her like it was something she suddenly didn't want, something that stunk to her, something to get rid of, and she was grateful the guy had in fact taken it from her and run in the other direction, as if he were the one being chased and was scared himself. *So now the sympathy express stops for everyone,* her husband will say, and then go further and accuse her of not understanding what had happened to them, of really just

THE PERIPATETIC COFFIN

not understanding, another liberal-leaning moment of not con-necting the dots, that he could've been killed for chrissake, and she will tell him *but you weren't, you weren't, you weren't* as he leaves the kitchen to double-check the doors and windows, whiskey in hand, walking briskly from one point of entry to the next, cupping his eyes against the glass to get a better sense of who might be standing outside, with his wife's keys, *he knows our address, did you think of that? Our address.*

That night, after she's put Sam to bed, after she's explained to him that *no, nothing happened to Dad, he just fell on some ice* and after Sam has accepted that explanation, and laughed at it even, because, at seven years old, slipping on ice is a probability—something he can understand though he has never actually *seen* his father slip—she will find her husband in their bed, remove her clothes, and join him. You understand, she will say, that you cannot get mad at me for this, and he will say of course. He doesn't know what he's thinking, of course he's not mad at *her,* he's just infuriated, and hurt, and these feelings have nowhere else to go. What do you need? she will ask him, and when he doesn't respond, she will complete this thought, and say that she needs him, that is what something like this shows you, that is the important thing, the only good part. They will try at sex but give up almost immediately. She is tender with him; he is lethargic with her. Their normal su-ture, gone. His eyes, still gone. They are, both of them, still walking back to their car in their minds.

* * *

In bed, later, with Charles miraculously asleep, on his back and snoring into the void, Claire will hear her son across the hall and realize she's been waiting for this, the moment of his waking, and has, in some way mysterious to her, willed it. Recently he has become afraid of everything—the way the wind ruffles the curtains, what the night does to the color of a picture hanging on his wall, loud cars and sirens—and when he is afraid he comes to her. She will hear the instant his eyes snap open, will hear him sit up in bed, whimper softly, and swing his legs to the floor. She knows, as he walks the distance between them, that in one hand he's carrying his pillow and with the other is dragging his blanket behind him like, Lord help her, this is how she thinks of it, like a bridal train, halfheartedly making his way to a sleepy ceremony. They've set up a rule: if he wakes he can come into their room to sleep for the rest of the night, but he cannot sleep in the bed with them; he can bring his blanket and he can sleep on the floor, next to her, so he will know she's right there, always. But boundaries need to be respected, even by seven-year-olds, perhaps *especially* by seven-year-olds, perhaps especially by *her* seven-year-old, who seems capable of accepting every emotion she can imagine, every emotion she pushes in his direction, without filling up. He is a planet-eater. With the exception of tonight, never once has he flinched from an embrace. Never once has he told her to leave him alone. It is a rule, tonight, she'll consider breaking.

He will wordlessly put his pillow on the floor, wordlessly

spread his blanket and lie down. She will reach for him, take his hand, and say *dreams?* He will squeeze her hand and she will feel an immense gratitude and he will say *yeah* and then take his hand from hers and return it below his blanket.

"Jesus *Christ,*" her friend Jill will say the next morning. "Did you call the police?"

"Charles didn't want to," Claire will say. She is in the bathroom, on the phone. Phone cord stretching from the kitchen.

"*I* would've called the police."

"He was *crying,* Jill."

Her husband will take the day off from work. The moment to talk about what happened to them, between them, is long past. His mouth is tender; in the mirror it looks sore, like the guy, whoever it was, had taken a fistful of cotton and jammed it in his lip and left it there. To his surprise he is pleased to see his face mildly disfigured, it makes him look not himself, as if a harder face had surfaced in order to give proper shape to the way he is feeling. His gums throb, pulse outward from an epicenter he locates in the middle of his palate. The pain, the mild pain, is radiant, and moves away from him like ripple-waves, bouncing off the bathroom walls, coming back to him never fully absorbed. He'll spend the morning driving around from hardware store to hardware store, looking for dead bolts, looking for window locks, talking to some kid in an orange apron about home security systems. He'll return with a sack full of metal, and spread it on the dining room table and stare at the pile, hands on his hips, a picture, to Claire, who is watching him from the kitchen, of someone reading fortune bones. She will walk behind him as he's sorting the pile, drape her arms around him and feel, at his side, under his lightweight jacket, something hard.

"Hunting knife," he'll say.

"You're wearing it around?" she'll say.

"I just bought it," he'll say.

"Don't you think that's a little . . ."

"*What?*" he'll hiss.

She'll be taken aback. She'll step away from her husband, and let him come to her. When he doesn't, she'll say, "What are you going to do? Get in a knife fight?"

"Did *you* get punched in the face?"

"He took my purse, remember. I was there too."

"I know you were there."

"What's next, a gun? Do we want that in our house? Are you going to let all of this into our house?"

"I'm protecting our family, Claire. It's pretty simple. Now, if you'll excuse me, I'm going to install some locks."

The house, locked, will feel different than before. The creaks louder, the plumbing worse. Every quirk an agitation. Four days after the attack, Saturday night, her husband will spend an entire evening driving around the neighborhood, flashing high beams into unlit corners. He'll walk back into the house and go straight upstairs. He'll inspect his lip for half an hour, just looking at himself in the mirror, while Claire reads Sam to bed. This, she'll remind him, is a night when they should be eating together. He'll say he had work to do, and she will let it slide. Two mornings later, while Charles is at his office, one of the newly installed locks will fall off the door and hit the ground with a sound like a table collapsing. She'll inspect the divot left in the wood floor by the falling lock, unsurprised.

"What'd you do?" he'll say when she reaches him at work to tell him about the lock.

"I didn't do anything, it just fell off."

"You did *something*."

While he's at work, she'll hire someone to switch out the locks. That night, in the kitchen, she'll tell her husband *something's wrong here* and he'll say *nothing's wrong here* and she'll say *you're not acting like yourself* and he'll say *maybe I don't like myself* and she'll tell him *these things happen* and *maybe he needs to talk to someone about it* and he'll say *well, isn't that just like you to think that* and that she has no idea what he's going through and she'll say *what on earth are you going through* and they'll be interrupted by their son, who has heard them from his bedroom, and who is sending wooden blocks down the stairs to get them to stop arguing.

* * *

She'll reach for him in bed, and he'll grab her hand and take a shot at flinging it across the room. *Don't you ever do that again* she'll say, and he'll say *I'm sorry, I'm sorry.*

On Friday, their son will come home from school, dropped off in front of their house by the bus, by the driver who, most days, is overly friendly, but today will drive away as soon as the doors close behind Sam, as if, she thinks, he's got more important things to do today than make sure there's someone around to welcome each weather-bundled child safely inside. She'll meet him at the door, take his backpack and half-eaten lunch, ask him about Ms. Sabotka, and listen as he lists in chronological order everything he did today, first snack time, then recess, then drawing, then cursive, then choosing the music everyone in the class would listen to, then computers. She'll ask him then if he still wants to go over to Patrick's house for a sleepover, Patrick, the son of her friend Jill, who is as loud as Sam is soft, the Patrick who has stolen his toys and was then made by Jill to sheepishly return them, the Patrick forgiven instantaneously by her son, as if his toys meant so much less to him than Patrick himself, since it was Patrick, she was told, who wrestled with an older boy who was taking Sam's money at school. *Of course, Mom* he'll say, and she'll wonder, on the car ride over, if she was right or wrong in detecting a note of irritation in his voice, in that word, *Mom.*

Jill will have tea waiting for her. The two boys will immediately run outside arm in arm, like European kids, she'll think, like boys still unembarrassed by their own enthusiasm for each other. Jill will ask her how she's doing, and she'll say *fine, fine* and then catch herself on the verge of saying more, but what, exactly, she doesn't know, except that it feels like something's been deposited in the back of her throat, and she's been walking around for most of the day in a dreamy nonawake state, replaying the evening in her head. *Oh, honey* Jill will say, and reach across the counter for her hand, and then *at least he only wanted your purse, you can thank God for that, and also that Charles was there because otherwise who knows?* But Charles *was* there, and it had *still* happened, and whatever it was that this sort of violet talking had meant, if it meant anything at all, was that he had been unable to do anything to stop it. *Which is not to say he should've tried, you should always just hand the stuff over, big deal* Jill will say, and Claire will hear herself saying *I know, I know.* But still, it was just one punch and he'd gone down, and did not get back up, and had not chased the guy across the street, and did not act the way she wanted him to act, and had, in fact, left it to her to resolve the altercation. Which she had done. And which, she thinks, she is now being punished for.

She can see the boys through the kitchen window, engaged in some game with obscure rules involving imaginary enemies, the two boys clearly on the same side, lobbing what she assumes are grenades over the fence into the neighbor's yard. One of them brings his hand to his mouth and bites like he's holding an apple and then drops it, alerting the other one of the calamity about to befall them *inside* their own bunker, and the two of them dive into the snow, covering their ears with an *oh, no!* that's audible even from where she's sitting. The tea is warming her hands, and she listens as Jill lists one complaint after another, about her mother-in-law, about uninvited guests, about their dog and how he only seems to shit when he's sure he's got the widest audience available, about their heating bill, which, now that Patrick knows how to adjust the thermostat, has become astronomical. She's heard all of this before. Jill, Claire will know, is just trying to cheer her up. Eventually, Claire will decide to go home. She'll walk outside as it's getting dark, and drop a kiss on her son's cheek that he'll make a big show out of wiping away. She'll tell him to remember to brush his teeth, *in circles, every tooth*, and then, after a final shrug from Sam and a good-bye from Jill, will get in her car and drive the five miles home without turning on the radio.

When she turns onto her street, onto *their* street, onto the street where all three of them live, and have lived for six years, she'll see that every light in her house is turned on and blazing, a beacon in the night, so bright there's a halo effect around the whole place. It looks, she'll think, like they've stolen all the electricity in the city. She will stop and park, walk on the sidewalk and pretend she's a neighbor, out for a stroll, and that this is not her house, but the house of someone she barely knows, but whom she is friendly with, someone with whom, every third Tuesday, she makes bad, cross-alley recycling jokes, someone who can be counted on to bring KFC to the neighborhood potlucks and sends the kids wild, but that's it. A good-morning here, a can-you-believe-this-weather there.

Nothing more than that. This house, now her neighbor's house, suddenly feels warm to her.

On the machine, there will be a message from her mother, and her husband will not be home.

"Well, *this* one was a gentleman, at least," her mother will say when Claire calls back. They've already talked about the mugging. Her mother is past it. No big deal. No one died. That's the main thrust of her mother's thinking, that no one died, so what's the problem?

"What do you mean by gentleman?" Claire will say.

"He opened doors! *Car* doors. He ordered for me. Swordfish. Which I'm not in the habit of eating, but I told myself: you *never* eat fish, but maybe you should. And I'm glad I did. They sprinkled nuts on it. He ordered steak for himself."

"Sounds wonderful?"

"But he's just so *old*. They're all so old. He shouldn't even be eating steak. I think he was showing off."

"You're not old."

"I'm older than you."

"That doesn't make you old. Are you going to see him again?"

"What else would I do? I don't know. He wants to get married."

"To you?"

"No, he didn't pro*pose*. But he did say he was in favor of 'cutting to the chase,' whatever that means."

"Gawd. Guard that chastity."

"And you," her mother will say. "Are you sure you're okay?"

This interest, the sudden turn in the conversation, will surprise Claire, and she'll not know, exactly, what to say. "*I'm fine. I didn't get hit.*" That's where she will start, and then she will tell her mother about the locks, about the driving around, about the knife, about how unacceptable all of it is, about how strange it can be to know someone and then not, but *strange* is the wrong word, the word she is looking for is more like: *unsettling.* Or frightening. Like you are strapped in the back of some car you think will stay on the road, but you can't see the driver's face in the mirror, or even if the driver is there at all. Or, like your husband is simply not acting like himself, her mother will say. That is true, she will say back. Not himself. And everything I do seems wrong.

"Claire, it was humiliating for him."

"It was humiliating for me. He's not handling this well."

Her mother will say she's sorry to hear it. And Claire will know she means it. But she'll also know her mother's true stance on all of this, because what her mother will come just short of saying is that if Claire is not careful, if she doesn't lead with sympathy, even at cost to herself, she will end up alone, just like her mother, going on dates, and talking about swordfish with strangers.

"Why are you sticking up for him?" Claire will ask.

"I'm not," her mother will say. "I'm sticking up for marriage."

* * *

After the conversation is over, after she's reluctantly hung up the telephone, *severed the connection* as her father used to say, and left her mother, alone, in the small apartment they helped her rent, Claire will walk the downstairs of her own house, calling for Charles on the off chance he snuck in while she was on the phone. The house, as she wanders through it—though it is bathed in light, or perhaps *because* it is bathed in light—will feel strangely uninhabited, will feel, and this is the only way she can think of it, like a movie set, with all these rooms just waiting, begging, to be inhabited by actors, and she'll find herself turning the lights out one by one as she passes through them. She'll return to the kitchen, and call Jill.

"Not there?" Jill will say.

"Not here. I think he's out looking for those kids. Or trying to save the neighborhood. Out on patrol."

"That's ridiculous."

"It's not ridiculous. He bought a knife, for God's sake."

"He's probably getting milk. Listen to yourself."

"He's not getting milk. How're the boys?"

"The house is at seventy-eight, they picked some boogers, and we ordered a pizza."

"Sam hasn't been sleeping well. I told you that, though, right?"

"Yes. You want me to send John over? Are you really getting freaked out?"

"No. I'm fine."

"Do you want to come over here?"

"No. Thank you."

She'll put the receiver down, listen for her husband, and wonder if she should call the police. And tell them what? That a week ago they had been mugged? That her husband has been acting like he's become trapped by a movie in his head, a version not of what did happen, but what should have happened? Is there anything at all the police could do at this point? On the fridge, there are notes, and photographs, and a couple baseball cards stuck on with magnets. A picture-strip of her and Charles, mugging for the camera in a photo booth, years ago, before Sam. And she's surprised to see, there in the picture, in his then-face, young, and exuberant, a glimmer of his now-face, hard set, distant, determined, unkind. As if this were the sort of man he had always planned to grow into.

Her husband, five blocks away, will be heading home. Coming toward him, a group of kids, a pack of kids, there must be ten of them, hooded against the cold. High school kids. *Little shits.* He makes up his mind to walk right down the center of the group and puts his head down until they come face-to-face and then he's suddenly flushed and nervous and despite himself, despite his resolve *not* to step out of the way, despite the fact that he's got some store-bought confidence sheathed in his pocket, despite the fact that he's been walking around all night looking for kids just like these, at the last moment he steps aside. *'Scuse you* one of them says. He'll mumble something in reply, and immediately regret it. *What?* one of them will say, turning around, clearly the leader, since the rest fall in line behind him. *Nothing. What? Nothing. Thought so.*

Claire, alone in the house, standing in the kitchen, will be visited by a memory she has of the vacation they took after she found out she was pregnant. They, the two of them, Claire and Charles, on their way to Maui, sparing no expense, and once there sparing not even themselves in the Hawaiian heat. The sun cooked through their low-SPF sunscreen almost immediately and forced them back inside to the hotel pool, where they lounged, dispirited, until they realized the beach umbrellas were rentable and rented one, and tromped back down to the ocean. They were in so much pain from the sun but couldn't stomach the idea of flying ten hours to *not* lie out on the beach, and so they spent the rest of the late morning wearing long sleeves, in the umbrella's shade. Around lunch, after two hours of baking, fully clothed, in the midday Maui heat, Charles had turned to her, wearing sunglasses and a Gilligan hat that barely provided shade for his zinc-painted face, and said in his father's voice: *well*, this *is money well spent*. It had made her laugh so hard—his face, she hadn't recognized it, neon-covered and smiling, an advertisement for some debacle vacation, and his voice so like his father's—that some of her virgin banana daiquiri had come through her nose. He had said *Claire, that is beautiful* and she told him if he didn't like what he saw, it was just his tough luck. He'd said *no, I like it* as he got up on his elbows, *I love it* as he stood and then fell on his knees next to her and said *I like it* and then, out of nowhere, like something out of a nature show, he had ducked in close and licked the tip of her nose. She was so surprised by this, and made so oddly happy, that she dipped her nose deep into her drink and told him to try again, and the two of them had made a spectacle of their love for each other. You don't fly ten hours to act like yourself, you fly ten hours specifically *not* to act like yourself, to rev whatever engines require revving, to get sunburned and silly, to not care, to really *not* care that you look like tourists with sun poisoning, or like two people trying to convince each other the decisions you made together were the right ones. Had there been anxiety about the pregnancy? There had been. But here they were: paradise. And it hadn't mattered the next day when the rain began, conjured up from who knows where and so relentless they dubbed it *parade-stopping,* because near the beach was a cabana, and after they'd braved the sheeting water found themselves sitting alone under its roof. They stayed for hours. And just as they took one last look at the ocean before turning back to the hotel, the wind knocked a coconut from its palm tree and the thing flew down to them and rolled across the cabana's slat floor. A hairy bowling ball, come to deliver the news. She had picked it up, and handed it to her husband, and told him *congratulations, it's a coconut,* and he had said *that's fine by me* and then after deciding it would be a girl and naming her, they'd taken turns reassuring each other they'd protect her from every bar-sponsored spike on the beach. Even if it *was* a coconut. Even *if* security, in coconut-land, couldn't be guaranteed, they told her that tonight, at least, was one night she wouldn't have to worry about thirsty tourists. They'd held the thing like a newborn, and enjoyed the expansive feeling they imagined this stranger would bring them, agreed that this stranger's intrusion would result only in a deepening of themselves. That was the promise, then. They'd agreed.

From the street, Charles will see his wife has come home. He'll see she's turned off most of the lights—the outside lights, the bedroom lights, the lights in the living room—but the kitchen lights are still on, and through that particular window, he can see her, leaning against the refrigerator, standing still like she's studying something *on* the refrigerator, unaware of everything else, standing posed, as if framed in a painting. She could be anyone's wife. He wishes she were anyone, at this point, *but* his wife. He'll reach down for some snow, pack a snowball, and underhand it at the window. She'll startle, and glance at the direction of the sound. She'll turn her body toward the window, and roll her shoulders forward, unsure of herself, and he'll know then that he loves her, but he can't help, or stop, himself. He's pulled his hood low over his face. He doesn't want to be recognized, even if, and this he doubts, she can see beyond her own reflection in the glass. He'll pick up a stick, chuck it onto the roof so it pinball-clatters between the gables, and be pleased with the sound. She won't take her eyes off the window. He'll reach down again, and pack another snowball; this one he'll toss overhand, aimed right for the center of the painting. He hasn't thrown like this since high school. He hasn't moved like this since before he knew Claire. He hadn't ever in his life been hit in the face, and this snowball is aimed directly at her face. It is flying perfectly. And directly before impact, the instant before the snowball flattens and Velcro-sticks to the window with its hollow thwack, the lights, in the kitchen, go dark.

dirwhals!

december 10

This evening near the end of our shift the sun cracked like a brilliant orange yolk over the horizon. Bushard was standing next to me at the rail, and I told him it reminded me of the radiant and cold northern sunsets of my youth. He conceded that it would be possible to see it as beautiful, if only he could forget that beyond the twilit sand we could see was an operatic expanse of more sand. If he could erase this particular moment in history, have chosen another industry, and could, in fact, be someone other than himself, he said, then yes: beautiful. I told him that was the uplift I'd been looking for. He shrugged and replied it wasn't his job to cheer me up.

Tuva, my sister, you know me! I am long gone; your anger is justified. I left you when I could have stayed, when you needed me most, and my guilt has tugged at me like a living thing as we've crossed these dunes, looking for the bounty we have slowly come to realize may no longer be here. My messages to you go unanswered, but still I write, as if to underscore my own solitude and give shape to this expedition. These notes are addressed privately to you as well as myself; I feel compelled to put everything down. Will you read them? Years from now, will any of this make sense? At the very least I hope to find a friend in this log; and if not you, then perhaps someone else will consider these jottings of note. Perhaps I will even find fame in an obscure journal of history. I'm dating these entries; there's no reason for everything to come to nothing. The light has gone, the room is asleep. Let's begin.

My name is Lewis Dagnew, low crewman and spotter aboard the shipper-tank *Halcyon*, a tight-sleeper in an iron fo'c'sle, and one of thirty men to cast our lots and try our luck amidst the rolling dunes and oppressive heat found in the territory known as the Desert Gulf of Mexico. We left terra firma—packed dirt—over a year ago, and came to pin our fortune on the sliding sands; a fevered prospect, thus far an elusive hope. In the *Halcyon*'s case, fortune means a full hold; and we are here, a million miles from home, surrounded by a basin of sand four thousand miles wide, for one reason only: to spot, lance, and render dirwhal, that sand-diving beast, that dirt-drinking mass, that oil-saturated slowpoke who gave rise to an industry that not too long ago supported the energy needs of the entire southern biosphere.

According to a normal timetable for an expedition like ours, we should've been off the sand months ago. Instead, we've pushed farther and farther out, treading concentric and ever-widening circles that place us well outside of the historically teeming hunting grounds. The heat during the day is constant and unyielding, the temperature yet to dip below 113 degrees, and our daily sweep has come to feel like a slow grinding scuttle across the floor of an arid oven. We've been issued sun-suits for the UV, but they do little to mitigate the heat. At the end of our deck shifts we go below, peel the heavy suits from our skin, and make jokes about being basted in our own juice.

We are, it seems, alone on the sand. In the galley there's a poster that explains how the pay structure works. It's titled: Envision Success. But there have been no true dirwhal sightings, no trumpet's call. Instead we compare heat-induced hallucinations of dirwhals breaching just off the bow and slipping back into the sand, never to be seen again.

In the early months, we glimpsed other shipper-tanks cresting over the far dunes, but at that distance it was unclear if they were friendly vessels or not. We steered clear, and they disappeared like memories. Tuva: I would say that this state of isolation and disappointment dovetails with my general constitution and the luck I've had so far in life. But I am resolved to think of this voyage as more than a series of setbacks, even as the majority of the crew has begun to fret about the apparent barrenness of our surroundings. I am not here to sound the depths of my self-pity; I am here to push past the vagueness of my limited accomplishments. This morning, Renaldo caught me holding this journal and suggested I bind the pages and title it the *Denouement*. But why not assume that tomorrow will bring us what we're looking for? Tonight I said as much to Bushard before lights-out.

"A dream is a wish your heart makes," he said, then turned his back to me and pulled his pillow over his head.

december 18

The *Halcyon* is a G Model 7 Kermode shipper-tank—one of the last in a series to roll out of Detroit before the invasion shut those factories down during my father's generation—equipped with modified sand-treads and a flat metal deck. We are a slow-moving factory, an ungainly vessel that serves both as a hunting ship and a one-stop bio-processing plant. Our bow curves like a shovel, and is weighted for equal distribution at the contact points with the porous sand that surrounds us. The bridge rises abruptly, perpendicular, straight up, and is well windowed to aid with spotting. Stem to stern measures 180 feet, the length of three full-grown dirwhals laid head to tail. Middeck there's a portable tryworks—three huge iron cauldrons perched atop industry-grade burners—where all our rending will theoretically occur. The cutting instruments—bizarrely curved, long-handled pole-knives so sharp you can't help but imagine slipping them through flesh—are lashed under the portholes for easy access.

From a distance, the overall impression the ship gives on the sand is that of a single and colossal iron shoe. Our hold, now empty, is a cavernous double-deck capable of storing the rendered bio-matter of anywhere between four to six hundred mature dirwhals. At four RPMs, the engine roar of the *Halcyon* is deafening; at six it's like confusion opening in your skull. Below deck it's a Minotaur maze of close corridors and low ceilings, poorly lit passageways that dead-end for no discernible reason. The buggy-steerers, mates, and coopers: they've each got their bunks aft, walls decorated with posters and postcards. Our Captain Tonker's got his king's quarters. The rest of us sleep in the bow near the engine, where there is little relief from the motorized churn of our generators.

Today the plan had been to send a small group out in the buggies to explore the grounds to the south of us. I had been eager to leave the ship, but at the last minute one of the coopers decided he wanted to go, and I was forced into another eight hours of watching the sand from the hoop-rig near the stern. The buggies—we have four of them, small six-wheeled dune crawlers, each equipped with shock-prongs and a large sand-visor—zipped over the sand and away from the *Halcyon* with the buzzing speed of small insects. No one waved.

Of the dirwhals I have yet to see I know this: they are large beasts, well toothed, long and finned, with a wide head that tapers to a flat tail, but their skin is the color of coal, which makes them easy to spot against the dunes. They have been known to attack shipper-tanks, but they are no match for the ordnance in our bomb-lances, and accounts of dirwhal aggression are at this point little more than spook stories, things of the past. It's possible they've evolved to fear and avoid us. It's more likely, though, that as their numbers have dwindled they have simply moved farther out into the basin, and as a result the hunting strategy aboard the *Halcyon* is straightforward: wherever they go, we follow.

In the spotter's manual, there is a color page delineating dirwhals by genus. Eight of twelve are crossed out, and two of the remaining four don't render into usable energy. According to the timeline provided, hunting began in earnest forty-seven years after the Shift—the same year the Gulf drained and Further North refroze—and it's taken us all of three generations to thin out what at first seemed an unlimited resource and the solution to all our energy problems. They are known to burrow under the sand to avoid the sun, but they sleep and feed on the surface. It's been established that running an electrical current through the sand rouses them, but each day we send buggies to plunge a charge, and so far the pronging has yet to reveal anything at all.

Months ago, I telecomped my sister—yes, you, Tuva—that things here weren't so different from home: no perceivable seasons, weather that drives you into yourself, the illusion of unlimited space, shifting loyalties, petty grievances that burrow and sprout unexpectedly into meadows of resentment. *That's nice of you to say,* my father comped back. I asked to speak directly to you, and he told me you weren't interested in coming on the line.

I could have insisted. I could have explained myself more

clearly. Instead I cut the connection. Later, Renaldo told me I had a message. It read: *Everything is worse.* I stared at your message for an hour, typing and erasing different versions of a single apology before giving up and resolving that tomorrow, or the next day, I would try again. I never did. Weeks went by. Months. And now I've been informed that we are out of range for communication with anyone outside of the basin.

Of note: there is no wind here in the Gulf, and the stillness is eerie. Yesterday, Renaldo mentioned that up in the hoop-rig, high above the deck and away from the engine noise, he had the sensation that we were the only moving thing for miles. It felt, he said, like he was the last man in the universe, cut loose from the earth, drifting through a painting.

january 15

This morning, Captain Tonker summoned all hands to the aft-deck. We gathered, and he stood above us on the bridge, brow furrowed against the sun. He's a terse man, not given to conversation. He's made it clear that he will brook neither dissent nor opinion. Those of us in the bow see him rarely. But what he had come to tell us was now that we were moving farther and farther into the basin, those on watch were to be spotting for two things: dirwhals, and other shipper-tanks, which, given our current location, would most likely belong to the Firsties. A collective groan, followed by hissing, went up among the crew. *Protection kooks,* someone explained to me when I asked who the Firsties were. Bushard added: kamikaze environmentalists; degenerates; cultists; criminals. Captain Tonker held up his hand for silence.

Their aim, he said, is to put us out of a job. Shipper-tanks have been dodging Firsties for years, and between them and Captain Tonker it's a pointed circle of antagonism. He went on to explain that as the number of dirwhals has decreased, the number of preservationists active in the dunes has tripled, and their aim is the disruption—sabotage—of expeditions like ours, either by the violent immobilization of licensed shipper-tanks or by provoking us into firing on them. The law is on our side, he said, but they care nothing for the law. He ground his fist in his palm, and asked us how we felt about such heartlessness? So, his order: spot the Firsties, and report them, but under no circumstances were we to engage, even if provoked. They had cameras, they wanted us to fire on them, and they would stop at nothing to manufacture an incident, even if it came at great cost to their organization. He asked us if we understood. We answered: yes, of course.

No one knows how old Captain Tonker is, but we know from the coopers that as a young man he'd been mate aboard a small fleet of shipper-tanks during the Great Hunt of '78: the hinge-creak moment when it became clear just how lucrative the dunes could be. He'd been aboard a buggy doing a routine sand-prong, and whatever charge they sent down roused the earth itself. An entire dirwhal colony came to the surface. The lances were still rudimentary in those days—plagued by poor penetration and ordnance malfunction—but it didn't matter: by the end of the second day, so much unrendered viscera had been spilled that his buggy had trouble finding traction in the sand. They were cutting and cooking for weeks. Flames licked the tryworks and illuminated the night sand, where the dead dirwhals were rolled together like pallets of log, awaiting their turn at the cutting platform. They were their own sun, a pulsar of energy that incinerated for twenty-four hours a day, and even so some of the dirwhals they lanced fell rotten before the buggies could pull them to the docks. The voyage had lasted all of two months, and taken them no more than two hundred miles into the Gulf. With the payout he got, he bought an island off the Canadian coast. Afterward he was made captain, and rechristened his ship the *Halcyon*.

"Ah, the good old days," Bushard said when he heard the story. "Renaldo, answer me this: where have all the flowers gone?"

Renaldo shrugged. "Tonker's got 'em all," someone said back.

Four weeks have passed since my last entry. Every day we wake up, scan the dunes from the deck of the *Halcyon* for movement, and see none. The only news delivered on Thursday came after Renaldo ran a lance check and discovered that half of them were temporarily inoperable on account of disuse. "That matters *why*?" Tom, one of the coopers, had the misfortune of saying as Captain Tonker emerged from the steerage. To our great pleasure, he was demoted on the spot; to our displeasure, he now sleeps with the rest of us in the bow. "Every downside has a downside," Renaldo told him when he complained that he was sick of sleeping with those of us he considered below his station. "Welcome to the melting pot."

january 29

Tuva, a question: How long do you stare at something before you realize it isn't going to change? How long before you understand your own misfortune to be something other than a series of bad breaks? Here is my memory of home: long, dark days; a small-efficiency trailer; an expanse of frozen tundra; my inability to set anything in the right direction; a growing desperation that would not quiet. During the winter we slept in our boots. Our father moved us there, following a job, from Vancouver: you were five, and I was six. Every morning, he kicked around the kitchen, then put on his goggles and one-piece and hopped the bus that took him to the upland digging grounds, where he worked on a crew that removed layers of barely melted permafrost using outdated and rusty scalping equipment.

When we asked him what he was doing there, he replied: digging a hole. Eventually the plan was to erect a rig and burrow the mantle for mineral reserves, but Standard had union problems, and the rig, always coming, never showed. The union called new arrivals like our father clod-kickers and line-breakers, and appeared to be happy to let our town crumble under the weight of its own hopelessness. People like our dad called the union guys motherfuckers, and sidled up to the bar to make plans of their own that always came to nothing.

Everything we owned was leased, and leveraged against an eventual payout. I spent my free time trying to avoid the other kids in town, who needed someone to pick on, and had chosen me. I didn't put up much of a fight. I flinched when doors shut. I slipped when running. My forehead was an oil slick. *You haven't spoken in four days,* my mother said when I was twelve. I corrected her, and told her it had been four*teen*.

But bad as it was for me, Tuva, I know it was worse for you. The upland diggers, most without families, wore their loneliness like wolves. You turned twelve, and our mother became distracted and agitated. You turned thirteen, and it was like all the air had gone out of the room. The other kids turned their attention from me to you. After you'd been groped at school for the umpteenth time, my mom took us to the principal. He *looked* concerned, but eventually shrugged, turned to me, and asked me where I'd been while all of this was happening. I showed him my torn jacket and a patch of bloodied scalp, and told him there was nothing I *could* do about it. *Well,* he said. He cleared his throat and made a gesture like his hands were tied. After that, my mom took you out of school, and forbade you from leaving our property after 4:00 P.M. Above the door to our trailer, there was a sign Mom had needle-pointed during one of her near-depressions. *Home Is Where the Heart Is* it read. I remember you hard kicking your boots on the steps. "Who needs a heart?" you said, before going inside.

It won't be like this forever, I told you. It's not so bad.

"For you," was your reply.

Then, when you turned seventeen, two grown men who

showed up at our trailer, demanding to see you. Our mother, through the door, told them our father would be back any minute. They said: We don't care. They swore, they kicked the door; eventually they left, said they'd be back. Mom called the police. They never came.

And where was I during all of this? Under the couch, with you, Tuva, holding your hand with my eyes closed from fear. And then, as soon as you could, you left.

I don't know what happened to you while you were gone, I don't know where you went. I only know that a year later, when you returned, your eyes had changed, and I left as soon as I was able.

march 4

Three days ago, a shout from the high-hoops roused us from sleep. Bushard spotted it: a shipper-tank, the first we've seen in months.

The ship—the *Waker 4*—was on her way back to the mainland, and our rendezvous was short. Over the last seven months, they'd seen a grand total of four dirwhals, of which they'd lanced two. Before that, they'd spotted, but not lanced, three. All told, they'd been on the sand for two years. They'd seen a cluster of Firsties but hadn't been confronted in any meaningful way. They'd been called home by their backer, who'd lost his shirt outfitting them and finally pulled the plug. Not that it mattered; by the time that call came in, both of their buggies had broken axles, the ship had flaked rust into their water supply, and the first mate had fallen deathly ill. The expedition was over. Twelve days ago, as they pulled line for home, they'd seen a few black-painted shipper-tanks patrolling the distant dunes, watching their retreat like gleeful crows.

I see now it's been five weeks since my last entry. February passed like a dream of heat. March is no better. We've seen no activity in the basin save for the crew of the *Waker 4*, which slipped out of sight the following morning like a ghost-ship, a mirage in the dunes. Our solitude is beginning to feel overwhelming. No messages go back and forth between us and the mainland. The sun-suits we've been issued seem to be near the end of their shelf life, with elbows threadbare and zippers filled with grit. I've developed a rash on my inner thigh, and have sewn extra fabric on the inside of my pants to ease the chafing and keep out the sand.

april 19

I haven't kept up here. I see it's been many days since my last entry. My rash has healed, leaving only slight discoloration across my leg. But Tuva: today was the day we'd given up waiting for, and an account seems not only necessary but verging on the joyous.

It began this morning with an alarm—one of the mates announcing he'd seen irregular sand activity off the stern. In no time it became clear that what he saw in the distance was no trick of the overheated mind, but an honest spout—a dirwhal's gritty exhalation; a playful fluke of dirt—and no sooner had we crowded the rail than the beast breached full, exposing its length before disappearing once more below the surface and burrowing a large and sucking indention in the basin's floor.

It was nothing short of chaos on deck. Half of us were without our sun-suits, the other half stood dumb and awestruck. This creature was enormousness itself, more viscerally alive and mobile than I'd thought possible. We watched as it surfaced again: a dark stain against the sand, winding its rounded bulk across the basin floor, rolling sideways rather than cutting in a straight line as I had always imagined it would move. I could make out its rear flukes against dunes as it dove again. There was a mad scramble for the munitions locker. There was banging, yelling; gear dropped; gear found. All the while, Captain Tonker stood atop the rear-deck shouting instructions into a megaphone that no one, in our rush not to be left behind, heard. Space or no we jostled into the buggies, were lowered from the rail, fired up the engines, and took off in the direction of the thing itself.

What was going through my head at the time I can't say. In my memory, oft replayed, it feels as if I were traveling through a tunnel, though we had been below open sky. Sand peppered my visor, and kicked up behind us in twin arcing flumes. Bushard was in one of the other three buggies. I held my bomb-lance to my chest, tip pointed overboard to minimize the damage caused by accidental misfire as we careered across the flat expanse. All of us leaned forward into the wind; everyone crowded the bow. The creature surfaced again, and this time lay atop the sand, as if sunning itself. And though we were moving as fast as the buggies would carry us, our progress felt excruciatingly slow. We all feared the same thing: that the monster would slip away quietly, never to be seen again.

When we were within darting distance, the beast dove once more, leaving a large, sand-sliding crater in its wake. We cut our engines. No one spoke. It was so quiet you could hear the sand running over itself as it filled the crater, a high-pitched desert whistling that brought to mind nothing so much as the wind-sound I remembered from my youth. I felt hot, but understood that the heat was inside my suit, was coming from me. My heart pumped as if I'd been running.

The order came to prong the sand. Tom jumped from his buggy, and drove the hollow aluminum staff into the lip of the crater. As soon as he was back aboard, one of the mates juiced it. There was an electric buzzing, the sand hopped, but other than that, nothing. The seconds passed like minutes. *Again,* someone shouted. The voltage was recalibrated, and the mate hit it again.

At that point there arose from the sands a muffled shriek, and from behind where we had parked came a sound like the earth squishing open. We turned in time to see the dirwhal leap his enormous bulk directly out of the sand. For a moment in his breach, he crossed the sun, hung in the air, and we were in shadow. Then he landed like a hammer of God directly on top of the second mate's buggy, which disappeared below his belly with a muffled and sickening thud of dust.

It's possible we heard the call not to fire. It's possible in our haste we ignored it. The moment before impact, I saw a flash of razor teeth, a perfectly smooth gullet; a breath-smell that was like ammonia wormed up my nose. Then twelve bomb-lances landed more or less simultaneously, and burrowed their tips in its skin. We had been instructed to aim for the head. In our enthusiasm, we did not. The bombs concussed; the center of the beast atomized into a red and white mist, and we fell back in wonder at what we'd done.

Immediately we'd known the chance of survival for our friends was negligible—if they had not been crushed and killed instantaneously by the dirwhal's crashing bulk, the explosion from our lances would certainly have finished them— but we also knew enough to try. Bushard and I affixed chains to the dirwhal's flukes. The mates hoisted the carcass onto the sled. As we moved that great body, we saw our three companions, half-buried in the sand. It was impossible to tell if it was their blood or the blood of the dirwhal we were seeing. That somewhere below the boredom of our expedition lay tremendous risk was something we'd forgotten, or stopped considering, or purposely ignored. Renaldo sat down hard in the sand. The rest of us removed what we could from the crushed buggy, zipped most of that in bags, and we set toward our ship. We were greeted by those still aboard the *Halcyon* as if we'd conquered Rome.

The cutting and rendering will last for the majority of the next few days, and will require all hands. Captain Tonker has scheduled a funeral for three days from now, and instructed that the remains of those lost be kept in cool storage. He mentioned that in all of his years on the sand, he'd never lost a member of his crew. It is difficult to tell if this has touched him in any way at all.

april 20

Too tired to relate much of the day. Everything is taking longer than it should, no doubt because many of us have never set foot on a cutting platform, let alone performed such grotesque surgery. Every part of the ship smells as if it's been brined with vinegar and putrid rot, a stench so overpowering and permanent seeming that we've taken to wearing our sun-suits below deck to mitigate the odor.

In order to render properly, the meat must be cut clean from the carcass and the flanks hoisted aloft. From there, the small cutters flay those strips into liftable squares, and feed them in correctly measured amounts onto the belt so the works aren't overwhelmed and are able to render at the appropriate temperature. The blue flame from the burner flowers at the base of the cauldrons and licks the sides with such ferocity that we have to ladle in shifts to avoid collapsing from the heat.

This evening Bushard, along with some of the other hands, expressed concern that something might be wrong with our catch. When Tom cracked the head-case, there'd been a hissing sound, which was followed by a geyser of liquid the color and consistency of cream long gone off. Everyone in the immediate vicinity became sick. Eventually the foul-spout subsided, but it took an hour for anyone to feel well enough to venture near the head in order to butcher it. There was discussion about whether the head would cook or not, given its strangeness; and if it *did*, whether it would contaminate the other batches when mixed in at the cooper's station. Captain Tonker, however, waved his hand, and told Bushard the next time he wanted to waste his afternoon, to come find him in his quarters, where he'd be taking a nap.

All things considered, everyone is in good spirits. Renaldo informed me that even though we're now in one of the farther circles, near the outer edge of the hunting grounds, for the last few days we've been receiving transmissions from outside the basin. I asked him if there were any messages for me. He shrugged, and said there was a backlog. When I checked myself, my box was empty. "No news is good news," Bushard told me. I nodded. I must have looked upset. "I'm just trying to help," he said, and walked away.

I've written to my sister with the news of our catch, and am now awaiting a response. I sit, now, in the galley near the telecomp, transcribing my thoughts in this log. For the last two hours I haven't written a word. Members of the crew come and go. Tuva, if only you would write I could fall asleep. It wouldn't even matter to me what you said. Describe your misery. Tell me about the cold. Call me a coward for leaving. Be angry at the world for providing you with a brother who could not protect you. Tell me you will never forgive me. Anything would be better than nothing.

april 22

Tradition holds that after an expedition's first catch, the mates and steerers buggy a mile from the ship and her illuminated works to make a show of celebration. In our case, it would also serve as a send-off to those we lost in the hunt. At dark, those of us remaining aboard gathered near the hoops and bow-struts to watch them go. At an agreed-upon signal, they crossed their lances, and fired into the sky. According to this ceremony, wherever the farthest dart lands is where we will find our next dirwhal.

Seeing this tonight, I became so full of emotion that I had to grip the rail to steady myself. It wasn't sadness for those we lost. It wasn't relief that we had finally begun our journey in earnest. It was odd and expansive, a mysterious state that turned almost as quickly as it rose, to the point where all I could say about it now was that it felt like pity crossed with exultation, and as the lances blazed up on the distant sand I pushed as far back in my memory as I was able and conjured an image of family happiness inexplicable even to myself.

"Watch my arm," Bushard said. I was holding it. I apologized, and made my way below.

may 20

Four weeks have passed since my last entry, and in that time a bout of misfortune has found the *Halcyon*. One of the coopers put the gris through a series of tests, determined it had in fact contaminated the batch, the whole of which was now unusable. In an attempt to find new hunting grounds, we've pushed farther out into the basin, into relatively uncharted sand, and as a result have had our first run-in with the Firsties. They appeared two weeks ago, three small and fast-moving shipper-tanks cresting over the dunes. Most of our crew were in buggies running charges miles to the south of us; those of us left aboard were not prepared to fend the Firsties off. They struck quickly and retreated. The damage was one inoperable buggy, a tar-bomb affixed to one of our treads that didn't fire, and a series of unwanted leaflets that were launched from a distance and rained over the deck. We are now posted on watch twenty-four hours a day to guard against further raids, but have yet to see any further evidence of their ships on the dunes. No tread tracks, no transmissions, nothing but the damage to our ship to indicate they had ever been here.

In addition: three days ago, one of the mates fell from the bridge while repairing navigational equipment, and was buried without fanfare.

The result is such that our spirits, having momentarily lifted, are now deeply plunged. Annoyance and chagrin, the twin poles of our previous and collective emotional lives aboard the *Halcyon,* have given way to a disgruntled fatalism that no one is proud of and no one can shake. Thus far our expedition has amounted to this: we lanced a sick beast, boiled him down, and poured him back into the sand. Talk in the fo'c'sle is of a cursed voyage—the lingering stench of the dirwhal our unlucky, haunting talisman—but even as that superstition is passed around out of boredom and desperation, we know better. Years ago, someone discovered that the dirwhals crowding the Gulf could be rendered into usable energy, and made a fortune. After that, anyone who was able to scrape a shipper-tank together and get backing made his way to the sands. After that, expeditions became longer, to account for the travel time it took to reach new hunting grounds. Now, a generation later, anyone who puts on a sun-suit and stands for hours on deck like we do is forced to confront what Bushard has recently taken to calling the natural limit of optimism—as in, what'd we expect? The history of the world is the history of diminishing returns. You hunt something to the verge of extinction, it stays dead. It's not a curse, it's history getting the better of us; it's simply time catching up.

Two days ago, someone taped up one of the Firstie leaflets on the back wall of the toilet-stall. It's titled: "It's Not Too Late to Take Responsibility for What You Are Doing." It encourages us to return home and join their cause as spokespeople. There's a contest going to see who can scrawl the most realistic-looking dick on it using only the letters provided.

"It does seem like something you wouldn't want to wrap your mind around, doesn't it?" Bushard said.

I asked him: Me in particular?

He shrugged, and gestured out the porthole to the empty sands, as if further proving a point that escaped me.

The plan, as far as it's been explained to us, is to continue the expedition until either a full hold or a mechanical problem turns us around. The terrain has changed. The yellow sands have given way to more orangeish, and packed, dirt. It's become noticeably hotter. Those who have been on hunts before are unsure whether we've gone beyond the pale, considering we are now outside of traditional hunting grounds altogether. "What pale?" Renaldo said at dinner tonight. "Were we ever even *in* the pale? Did I miss an important part of this expedition?"

"Dirwhals are people too," someone said in a basso profundo voice. "Dirwhals. Are. People. Too."

june 18

Heavenly days: a phrase my father took to saying on reflex when confronted with news he didn't want to hear. *Heavenly days,* as he was cut from his logging job and moved us up north, trading one untenable situation for another. *Heavenly days,* as the rig was continually delayed. *Heavenly days,* when we woke up with half an inch of ice on the inside of the windows of our trailer, and my mother broke the glass trying to chip it off. *Heavenly days,* as the walls began to shrink and groan and we turned on him for his inability to see our situation for the thin soup it was: increasingly hopeless, wrecked, dead-ended, and dangerous.

He'd learned it from his father, who'd worked his whole life aboard a rig in the tar-sands until he was sent home with an evaporating pension and a breathing problem. *Heavenly days.* You say it right, it comes out as an expression caught somewhere between surprise and an acceptance of the inevitable— simultaneously the cushion to absorb the hammer blow, and the hammer blow itself. *We can't stay here,* my sister whispered to me through a hole she'd cut in the partition that separated her space from mine. She'd been crying. *Something will happen, don't worry,* I'd told you, because I could think of nothing else to say.

On account of the difficult terrain, Captain Tonker has limited the amount of ground the *Halcyon* covers on any given day. He's split the crew into discrete units, each responsible for the maintenance and upkeep of one of the ship's buggies. Every morning we're sent out widely in different directions for recon; as we hit designated areas, we run shocks into the sand to see what turns up. Nothing ever does. This afternoon, we buggied so far out we lost sight of the *Halcyon* completely. "Would it be such a bad thing," Renaldo said, after our third prong did nothing besides bring clods to the surface, "if we just drove this buggy home?"

When no one responded, he folded the map one of the mates had handed us into a small paper crane and flicked it into the basin. Then he apologized, and retrieved it.

Formally we've been told our supply of food will last another two years without restock; at our current budgeted fuel expenditure, we're looking at another three. Four days ago, one of the engineers mentioned that the shipmaster at the loading dock had pleaded with Captain Tonker to leave some supplies for the rest of the fleet; his response had been to fire the engines and wave the guy off. Those of us in the bow are in caustic awe of the foresight evident in this display.

Tomorrow will mark the 150th anniversary of the first

dirwhal sighting. At the urging of the second mate, the coopers have planned a comical reenactment of the scene, complete with sewn costumes and an impersonation of Captain Tonker, who was not there in body, but was in spirit. It's more the *idea* of Captain Tonker, we've been told. A broad sketch. Someone has hand-drawn playbills and passed them around. The play will be called: *I Was There at the Beginning: An Industry Is Born.* Under the title, there's a ferocious-looking dirwhal, drawn with human hands, holding the business end of a bomb-lance to its own head.

"I'm front row on this," Renaldo said when he saw the bill.

"Save a seat for me," Bushard replied.

june 19

Tuva: this afternoon, finally, I received your message. Is it the only one you've sent? Have you sent more, and have they been lost somewhere in the gulf that separates us now? In this message you asked if I remembered much about the time before we moved. Your only memory, you wrote, was of an afternoon at a public swimming pool that either you'd dreamed or had, in fact, existed on the first floor of our housing complex. We stood, the two of us, near the edge of the water. I'd been afraid to jump but said I would follow you, as soon as I saw it was safe. You didn't know how to swim, but felt there wasn't a choice in the matter: it was jump, or disappoint me. You jumped, and sank. Eventually the lifeguard pulled you out, sputtering and heaving for your own life. And when you opened your eyes, you saw that I hadn't moved from the edge. Your question: was that something *I* remembered too?

I went to answer, but the line was down. One of the mates informed me that the telecomp was on a delay. It was impossible to say when your message had come in. My options were to either record something, and on the next signal it'd be sent out, or continue to stare at the machine, looking like the world had ended.

"You know those people who blame everyone else for their problems?" Bushard said later, when I complained to him about the state of our transmission equipment. "You're those people."

I asked him: Who else *should* I blame? He replied that at least I was in good company here in the fo'c'sle: our own iron den of inequity and complaint.

"Cry about it," someone said, from the bow.

"That's the spirit," Bushard said back.

Last night I had a dream that rather than treading in wide circles, we were being pulled in a straight line across the desert by a cord that was visible only at night. The dark, sloping ridges in the distance shrank rather than grew as we approached. In my hands I held my visor and sun-suit, and was panicked to find myself topsides without my lance. I turned to someone I thought was Bushard, and was surprised to see it was you, Tuva, who had joined me on deck. You handed me a bowl of soup, and then another. My gratitude was overwhelming. As I went to thank you, you turned your head so I was unable to see anything but your hair and the side of your face. When I woke, I was weeping. Someone in the bow found this funny, and I stood, ready to pull whoever it was apart at the seams. It took four people including Bushard to calm me down.

july 7

Three weeks have passed since my last entry. There have been no further sightings of the Firsties, nor any evidence, anywhere, of dirwhals. We seem to be following a circuitous path conjured by a divining stick. The map of our progress— until someone finally pulled it down in frustration—resembled a fever dream drawn on an Etch A Sketch. The heat, as we've motored on, has become increasingly oppressive. When not on deck, we stand below in shifts directly in front of the cooling units, wicking the sweat from our bodies with towels nearly rancid from use. The engineers have expressed concern about wear on the injector cones, which haven't been serviced since we left and cannot be now, considering that in order to even *see* them properly, the whole shipper-tank would have to be taken apart. As a result, the engine now hums at a pitch that is just shy of earsplitting if you stand near a vent. Periodically, the sound of metal grating metal shoots into the fo'c'sle with enough force to make those unlucky enough to not have remembered their plugs dizzy with nausea.

To the question of what our collective hopes are for the rest of this expedition, I'd say our answer is plain enough: we just want to get off the sand with what, after two years, we feel we've earned. We came here to do something very specific, and simple; something many have done before; and the fact that we still sit on an empty hold feels to us like the retraction of a promise, the very definition of unfairness. It's a loaded deck, a cosmic rout of lousy timing. No one wants to be among the last ones on the sand, the suckers who stayed to turn out the lights.

"It's a feeling," Bushard has said, "I find impossible to describe." He was sitting at a table in the galley, with his head in his hands.

Renaldo asked him: You mean that it's happening, or that it's happening to *us*?

He closed his eyes. "I'm going to stop talking to everyone aboard this ship," he said.

august 2

Tuva, over the course of this expedition, I have come to understand what it is like to spend your life waiting for a rig that was never going to show. Time passes, the ship never comes in; at a certain point the ruined narrative solidifies, the hidden smallness and stupidity of your ambition presents itself in toto, and there you are: a walking avatar of foreclosed possibility. It's a dark understanding that one day is there like a weight on your neck. But nothing is written, and there's room for surprise. Opportunity can hulk itself from the dunes at the very moment you least expect it.

And today: the call on-deck sounded; our engines cut. We lined the port rail. The sun hit my visor like the idea of a headache spreading itself across the sand. I saw nothing. I asked what the commotion was about. Renaldo pointed.

In the far distance, a black speck. Then the sound of an engine. And then it hove more fully into view: a new model shipper-tank, outfitted with heat-reflective panels, a fly-bridge, and a full hull set atop a sleek, continuous track that made our own treads look like sand-churning windmills. As it came closer, however, it became apparent that all wasn't well: one of their stacks was shredded, there were char marks up and down the iron sheeting on her wide bow. Someone had painted over the name of their ship, and scrawled a dripping *Homeward Bound* just below. The crew stood on deck, facing us. As they passed less than a hundred yards of sand separated us and we formed a brief mirror-image, a silent communion that was broken only when they finally signaled for a conversation between captains, and Tonker retired to his cabin to initiate the transmission.

They were not Firsties, that much was plain. A smell of biological mustiness carried on the wind registered immediately. "They're riding low," Tom said. In fact, they were struggling to push through the sand. "You think?" Renaldo said back. Bushard tried to yell across to the other ship, but was met with silence. Their sun-suits were white, and reflected the afternoon light. They looked like ghosts, hovering at the rail. "Happy ghosts," someone said.

We stayed at the port rail, unmoving, for half an hour. Our new friends did the same. There was talk of disembarking on the buggies, but one of the mates hushed that idea before it took hold. Finally, with a lurch, our engines fired to life. The wheel was turned, and we made a slow arcing seventy-

THE PERIPATETIC COFFIN

degree shift to the west. The stern of our sister ship gradually moved out of sight, her tremendous bridge winking a final time as it passed behind a low ridge of dunes. Captain Tonker explained later: the *Homeward Bound* had found an entire pod of dirwhals, and was returning home with a full hold. There had been trouble with the Firsties, the ship was on her last legs, but they would make it off the sand.

He continued: and they have given us a parting gift—the coordinates for their proven but unsanctioned ground.

Tuva: this is a gesture rarely made between the captains of shipper-tanks. Our hope is restored. We've been instructed to spruce up the buggies and ready our equipment. Along with Bushard and Renaldo, I've pulled an eight-hour shift in the high-hoops. All told we'll be hoisted two hundred feet off-deck. As the stand was erected and we were strapped in, someone made a joke about the view. "Repeat that, please?" Bushard said.

"He said you look like three flags hoping to surrender," Tom said.

"Tell him where to stand so it catches him in the face," Renaldo said, as the motorized winch clenched and drew us heavenward.

The view from the hoops was staggering. I could see the sloping vanishing point of the sand in all directions, as if someone had gently pressured the horizon into a rounded dome that didn't so much meet the sky as push into it. The sound from engines below didn't reach our ears; their churning presence was apparent only in the vibration carried on the stilts between our legs. Everywhere I turned, the granulated vista appeared both limitless and small. In my happiness to find myself where I was, I reached for my notes and accidentally dropped my binoculars. They fell to the deck like a shot-down plane.

"Good Lord," Renaldo said. "Is there anything you *can't* do?"

august 18

Sighted over the last two weeks: fourteen spent lance casings; two sliding holes in the sand, which were speckled and strewn with sun-hardened biological matter; one burned-out buggy that after brief inspection was determined to belong to the Firsties; three discarded sun-suits; various instruments used to measure deep-sand activity; and a collapsible reflective tent.

We are now treading in a straight line to the west, following the coordinates we've been given, and moving well away from what could be called even substandard hunting conditions. The sand sits atop a stratum of irregular rock formations, glacier-cut a millennium ago, which in segments have been exposed and balded by the wind, the presence of which is in itself a novelty, considering the overall stillness of the Gulf. Two days ago we woke to a silent engine and a sound like waves crashing on the hull only to be told we were in the middle of a windstorm; when it was over, and the engines were fired once more, the sand-drift had climbed to the portholes on the starboard side. The extra care we are taking with our navigation has made our progress feel incremental.

If not for the evidence so plain in front of us, we would

surely be demoralized. But it seems that every time one of us is ready to admit that we perhaps have been led astray by some cruel practical joke played on one captain by another, a call comes in from the hoops or the buggies that points undeniably to the aftermath of a successful hunt as well as a confrontation between shipper-tanks. All crew on deck have been ordered to remain within spitting distance of a loaded bomblance at all times.

Bushard's mood has soured dramatically since our encounter with *Homeward Bound*. This morning he asked me if he was alone in thinking that what we were doing was, perhaps when all was said and done, a bad idea. When I asked him what he meant, he said: the whole picture—the pursuit of finite resources, the Firsties, the families hoarding their wealth in the southern biospheres, the burning wheel of industry, our participation in it. I told him that as long as I could remember I'd been too busy regretting what hadn't happened to think much about what might. From where I was standing, at least we were going *somewhere*. He looked at me as if I'd missed the point. I asked him: try again.

"Never mind," he said, and walked away.

august 20

This morning, we sighted two desiccated and partially blown-open dirwhal carcasses. In their state of decomposition, we were unable to tell their genus. Everyone, as we've pushed farther on, has grown antsy, agitated. The sand is waffled with deep and veering tread-tracks. It's increasingly clear that whatever went on here was less a deliberate lancing and more of an indiscriminate unleashing of explosives. We've been sent out in buggies for exploratory pronging, but none of those trips have turned anything to the surface.

"It's a dead end," Tom said at lunch. He was pushing the food on his plate into little mounds. "They've bombed everything out of the sand."

"Everything they could *see* out of the sand," someone said back.

After dinner, Captain Tonker called for an all-hands assembly at the stern to tell us that within four days we would reach our destination, and in order to be fully prepared he would be pulling down the high-hoops and clearing the deck of all debris not directly related to rendering. In addition, all but two of the buggies would be lashed to the interior rail until further notice. For those of us who didn't follow, it was explained to us that all lancing would occur from the deck of the *Halcyon*. What the captain of *Homeward Bound* had shared with him was that less than twenty-five miles away from where we stood now was a naturally occurring cove in the sand, ringed by tall ridges of rock. It would be there, if anywhere, that we would find what we were looking for, and our plan is a simple one: park ourselves in the mouth of the cove, juice the prongs, and fire as the beasts revealed themselves trying to escape.

"Easy as that?" someone behind me said.

"Easy as that," was Captain Tonker's reply.

Tuva: it brings me no pleasure to write that either the information provided by *Homeward Bound* was faulty, or we have, somewhere, somehow, veered off course. After four days, we saw nothing but hard sand in all directions. On the fifth day, Tonker ordered all buggies to resume patrols to the west and south of our current position. This morning, one of the engineers reported that the injectors had slipped their casing, and were now chafing against the lug-valves, which, considering those valves had already been sheered from continuous use, spelled a problem if we were at all interested in getting home. When asked how large a problem, he shrugged and spread his arms, as if measuring a large box he couldn't quite reach around. One of the mates asked him if he was sure. "I *might* be," he replied, then disappeared back into the engine room.

Further complication: while on a short recon patrol, one of the buggy crews has had a run-in with a group of Firsties, the first we've seen in months. As I write, they are on their way back to the ship with two of them. Either the Firsties had been on foot, or had left their own buggy camouflaged somewhere in the sand. The good news: we're convinced they can tell us something we don't know about the location of this cove, and their encounter with *Homeward Bound*. The bad news: lurking somewhere close is the rest of their crew.

Renaldo was on a different buggy, which, in light of the contact made, was called back. He reported there was nothing, absolutely nothing on the surface to see. The buggy carrying the captured Firsties is expected to arrive two hours from now.

Our engines have been shut off for an undetermined amount of time, and we're sitting deep in the sand. The silence, though shot through with expectation bordering on panic, is a relief. Bushard has just reminded me that yesterday, August 28, was your twentieth birthday. When I asked him how *he'd* remembered, he reminded me I'd asked him to do so, five days ago. I am losing the thread of our expedition. I feel I have lost the thread of everything. But what should I have done? No messages go through from here, of that I am certain.

august 29; evening

At first the boys—there are two of them—told us they were alone on the sand. Then they said that just beyond the ridgeline, there was an entire fleet of repurposed shipper-tanks, which would be coming for us shortly. Then they stopped talking altogether. We'd hauled them on deck as soon as the buggy docked. They were raggedly dressed, but wore matching boots and outdated sun-visors, dark green jackets that even in their threadbare state lent a military impression to their overall appearance. Neither looked to be older than eighteen. One of them, the smaller one, didn't have much English, and apparently stuttered when under duress. The larger looked even more frightened. One of the coopers had zip-tied them together at the wrists, so they were back-to-back with each other. Captain Tonker approached and asked if they'd been mistreated.

When they said no, he punched the little one in the sternum. "Not yet, you mean," he said.

They were separated for questioning. We were told to hold the tall one, and not let him out of our sight until Captain Tonker called for him. The other guy, still catching his breath, was pushed below deck with Captain Tonker on his heels. Bushard called for water. When no one moved, he went to get it himself.

While he was gone, no one said a word. Eventually the kid slumped over, and sat cross-legged with his back against the rail. His hair was cut short, and a small scar wound around his chin like a piece of white thread I kept wanting to wipe away. At some point Bushard returned with the water. The kid politely held up his hand and waved it off.

"I've got a question," Renaldo finally said. "And that question is: what are you even doing out here in the first place, protecting these things?"

The kid looked down at his lap, adjusted his hands. "Someone has to," he said. "They're on the verge of extinction. They've got nothing else."

Renaldo asked him to look around. He said: this whole basin is the embodiment of nothing else. It touches nothing at all. "That is where we part ways, philosophically," the kid said.

"So how many shipper-tanks have you destroyed?" Tom said.

"That's just a small part of what we do," the kid said back.

"From where I'm sitting, that's *all* you do," someone behind me said.

The kid closed his eyes, as if no matter what came next we'd simply agree to disagree. "This is illegal, you know," the kid finally said. "This ends it for you."

Renaldo grabbed the cup of water from Bushard, set it down, and told him we had him on that one. Legal or illegal; teeming or desolate sands: our hold was empty. This expedition had never even started for us. So he could save his industrio-accountability speech for someone on the winning end of that particular stick. The kid reached for the water, and said he'd keep it in mind.

Suddenly there was a scramble middeck. Word got passed that we were to take our temporary guest to the galley, zip him to a table-bolt, and suit up. As we made our way below, the engines roared with an unholy and squealing intensity, then settled into chugging life. Later we heard what everyone else apparently already knew: that Captain Tonker had squeezed some knowledge out of the stuttering Firstie, and that the cove we were looking for was less than seventy miles away. "Birthing grounds," one of the mates said as he inspected our lances. "A hotbed."

"Heavenly days," I said, and slapped Bushard on the back.

"Imagine that," he replied.

august 31

Tuva, it took two days on our full-throttled engines before we spotted the walls of the cove. At first these walls were a speck on the horizon; as we pulled closer, their sheer size became more plain. They rose darkly out of the sand; smooth, deep red and sun-baked rock formations high enough to cast long shadows across the dunes. A fortress rising out of the basin, glacier cut millennia ago. They must have formed a ring four miles around. If we hadn't seen it ourselves, we wouldn't have believed such a thing existed.

During the night, we'd run through our equipment, checking and rechecking cartridges, sharpening cutting tools. Captain Tonker had informed us that we would most likely meet resistance in the cove. He asked us if we were prepared to face this Firstie opposition like the men he knew we were. We nodded. We trial-fired our lances off the rail in unison, enjoying the sand-muffled concussion. Someone asked if the whole point was to *not* draw attention to ourselves, and as a thank-you for expressing concern he was sent below to mop the latrines. As the sun broke over the sand, though, we spotted two shipper-tanks in the far distance. They were dots off the stern, half a day behind us. Captain Tonker gave the engineers permission to try harder in the grease room, and ordered Bushard and me to bring the two Firsties on deck so their presence aboard would be more visible. As we zipped them to the rail, the smaller one saw where we were headed an instant before his friend did, and became inconsolable. Renaldo stuffed a face towel down his throat.

As we neared the mouth of the cove, one of the mates called for positions. I hitched my leg over the rail, next to Bushard, and eased my finger over the trigger-guard on my lance. The sun was merciless; we felt no different. The glare and heat off the sand shimmered a water-mirage on my visor. I felt one of my ears pop, and then the *Halcyon* made a sharp, arcing turn, moving us into the shadow of the high stone, and we came to rest perpendicular with the mouth of the cove, using our ship to block the opening.

Set up near where rock-base met the sand was a ring of small tents. I counted four or five unmanned buggies, parked in the shade next to what looked like a copse of monitoring equipment. Half of the large cove was gridded with wire, which divided the calm sand into rectangular segments measuring roughly fifty by one hundred yards. The other half appeared untouched, even by wind: not a tread mark, not a divot, not a single rake stroke. We stood at the rail for what felt like a small drop of eternity, expecting something to happen. Nothing did.

Bushard cleared his throat. "Would I be forgiven," he said, "for saying this feels just about right?"

Before I could answer, a man appeared through the flaps of one of the tents. Carefully, with his hands raised and with some evident discomfort, he began limping toward us. Without his sun-suit, wearing only a vest and some sort of wrap around his waist, he looked like a lost shaman, comically out of place. "That your dad?" someone said to one of the Firsties, and got no response. When the man was within shouting distance, he stopped, and pointed. We followed the line of his finger. Scattered along the top of the rock walls were groupings of other men, who looked just like him, also unarmed. As if by witness alone they could prevent us from doing what we came here to do.

Bushard put his hand on my shoulder, and nodded in the direction of the tents. A small dirwhal, the size of a buggy and lighter in color than the one we'd lanced, had surfaced and was winding its way toward our ship. It didn't know enough not to.

The man cupped his hands around his mouth. Whatever he yelled was lost over the scream of our engines. Another small dirwhal surfaced behind the first, as if it didn't want to miss whatever was happening. One of the men on the hill picked up a stone and chucked it down at us. It bounced harmlessly off the bridge. "I think," Bushard said, "they're urging us to reconsider."

"I would imagine so," Tom said, lifting his lance to his shoulder.

The *Halcyon* lurched further into position, wedging herself more firmly in the mouth of the cove; then someone cut the engines. Renaldo mentioned that the men on the ledge were hoisting a camera of some sort on their shoulders. I didn't see it. I didn't care.

But would it be going too far to say that as Captain Tonker gave the order to prong the sand and run a charge I felt a fleeting but deep pang of regret? As the sand began to hum with electricity, and the man, rather than running, fell to his knees, as if overcome by a great sadness, I wanted to tear at him for his stupidity and devotion. He knew—somewhere he must've known—this would happen; that we, or someone like us, would circle and eventually crest the dunes to take what remained from this cove. It was nothing he could stop. Bushard, next to me, gripped his lance like it was a lifeline. Next to him the two Firsties who had led us here strained at the rail, shielding their vision, and begged for someone to help.

Tuva, years ago now, I sent a message home that indicated the scenery here could be stunning: a desolate expanse shot through with an almost alien beauty. The dunes ridged in the distance, slipped their angles, and re-formed. The ground, far from being frozen, gave and depressed with each step. The sun hung in the sky and at certain hours lent the sands an appearance of a gold and undulating ocean. My intention then had been to show you that there was a world outside the one you knew. I know you received it, because in response you sent back a picture of your closed and locked bedroom door. And I know, now, that you were right. Tuva: I felt the lance kick against my shoulder. I reloaded, and fired again. For two years we'd thought ourselves the victims of history, but as we stood at the rail and marveled at the live sand below us, we'd become something else: a punctuation mark; the coffin's nail; agents of endurance, memorable only to ourselves. I aimed for the surfacing beasts, and eventually, aimed for the men who fired back at us. We sent the bulk of our explosives into that cove, squeezed water from stone, and nothing, no one, dug out.

acknowledgments

I'd like to thank the Minnesota State Arts Board, the Mc-Knight Foundation, and the Jerome Foundation for their generous support during the writing of this book.

A number of these stories are based on historical events, and I'd like to acknowledge two works in particular that provided the initial spark for some of the stories in this book. "The *Saint Anna*" owes much to *In the Land of White Death* by Valerian Albanov, and "The Peripatetic Coffin" found its footing only after a reading of *Confederates Courageous* by Gerald F. Teaster. Eventually fiction took over, and facts were bent, and broken, and used against their will, but I'm deeply indebted to the work of these two authors.

I'd like to thank Russell Perreault, Sloane Crosley, and Nayon Cho. Charles Baxter, and Julie Schumacher. Jim Shepard. Shelly Perron, and Martin Wilson at Ecco.

I'd also like to thank the editors of the journals where these stories first appeared, particularly Jill Meyers, Stacey Swann,

Devin Becker, Max Winter, Peter Wolfgang, David Daley, Hannah Tinti, and Marie-Helene Bertino. And of course, Alice Sebold.

I sometimes have nightmares about what these stories would have looked like without the fine attention and editorial suggestions of Libby Edelson at Ecco. And nothing at all would have happened were it not for Sarah Burnes at The Gernert Company. Thank you both. Toby, Carol, and Joyce: Three Lives & Company was for years my home away from home, and you guys my family. Paul Yoon and Matt Burgess: thank you isn't nearly enough for all the work you put into helping these stories along, but thank you just the same.

Mom, Dad, and Anne: my three favorite people.

And finally, finally: Maryhope. I should get you a T-shirt that says *I put up with all of this for years and all I got was a lousy book dedication.* You're the greatest. And I'm the luckiest guy around. Finally and always.